MW01254705

UFO CHRONICLES OF THE SOVIET UNION

A COSMIC SAMIZDAT

ALSO BY JACQUES VALLEE
PUBLISHED BY BALLANTINE BOOKS

CHALLENGE TO SCIENCE

ANATOMY OF A PHENOMENON

THE ALIEN CONTACT TRILOGY:

DIMENSIONS

CONFRONTATIONS

REVELATIONS

UFO CHRONICLES OF THE SOVIET UNION

A COSMIC SAMIZDAT

Jacques Vallee

in collaboration with
MARTINE CASTELLO

BALLANTINE BOOKS
NEW YORK

Copyright © 1992 by Jacques Vallee

All rights reserved under International and Pan-American Copyright Conventions. Published in the United States by Ballantine Books, a division of Random House, Inc., New York, and simultaneously in Canada by Random House of Canada Limited, Toronto.

Maps and illustrations rendered by Patrick O'Brien

Library of Congress Cataloging-in-Publication Data
Vallee, Jacques
UFO chronicles of the Soviet Union : a cosmic Samizdat / Jacques Vallee in collaboration with Martine Castello.
p. cm.
Includes index.
ISBN 0-345-37396-0
1. Unidentified flying objects—Sightings and encounters—Soviet Union. I. Castello, Martine. II. Title.
TL789.V348 1992
001.9'42'0947—dc20 91-55504
CIP

Designed by Ann Gold
Manufactured in the United States of America

First Edition: March 1992

10 9 8 7 6 5 4 3 2 1

SAMIZDAT: A DEFINITION

Samizdat is a Russian word for a document that is secretly copied by individuals to be circulated among trusted friends. For a long time, the works of Solzhenitsyn and Pasternak circulated in samizdat form. So did many Western works that were not approved by the government, including books about UFOs and parapsychology.

The situation in the former Soviet Union is changing, but even today the major sources of documentation on this subject are barely readable carbon copies of the reports and commentaries that a few dedicated Soviet researchers have been collecting. This book is a tribute to their perseverance and courage.

ACKNOWLEDGMENTS

In January 1990, in the opening days of a new decade, I had the opportunity to take an extraordinary journey to Moscow for an unprecedented series of meetings with the major researchers of the UFO mystery in the Soviet Union.

As anyone who has traveled there knows, nothing happens easily or by chance. My trip with Martine Castello was no exception to that rule. Therefore we have many people to thank for helping us make this voyage of exploration a successful reality. Primary among them are our families, who gave us the support we certainly needed as we embarked from Charles de Gaulle Airport on a bleak winter day.

On the Western side, our colleagues in high technology and journalism encouraged us to attack the many obstacles that seemed to block our way. Without the active support of Louis Pauwels and Philippe Jost at *Le Figaro*, the most basic arrangements could not have been made. The fact that we could travel to the Soviet Union under the flag of the most widely read newspaper in France opened many doors.

On the Soviet side, we are most grateful to the officials of Novosti and to our interpreters—Genya and

Serge in particular—who braved the difficulties created by our ignorance of their country, as well as the complexities of their own system, to make our stay in Moscow enjoyable and productive. In particular, Vice-Chairman Vladimir Milyutenko gave us unprecedented access to a wide range of officials and representatives of the Moscow media and of Soviet technology. It is thanks to him, in particular, that we had the opportunity to meet with Vladimir Migulin, who occupies the chair of radiophysics at the University of Moscow, and with several other esteemed Soviet scientists.

We treasure the new friendships we were able to establish among Soviet UFO experts during our visit. Professor Vladimir Azhazha was kind enough not only to answer our questions about his research but to organize a very gracious dinner at his home in Moscow to permit us to extend our conversations with his associates on an informal basis. Cosmonaut Valentin Zudov took time from a busy training schedule to explain the purpose and structure of the City of the Stars and the complexities of the Mir space station. Science writer Alexander Kazantsev received us graciously at his home, as did parapsychologists Eugene and Larissa Kolessov, two representatives of the Soviet New Age. Boris Churinov and his associates at the Twenty-First Century Group in Moscow provided a source of excellent data and good advice. Dr. M. Chevtchenko, mathematician Serge Bozhich, and other scientists helped us to become oriented in the rich and bewildering world of Soviet UFO research.

To those field investigators and researchers from remote regions who made a special effort to attend our conferences in Moscow—Professor Alexis Zolotov, who came from Kalinin; mining engineer Emil Bachurin, who came from Perm in the Urals (a two-hour flight); and the representatives of the Voronezh collective (engineer Alexander Mosolov, chief engineer Vyacheslav Martynov, and Dr. Yuri Lozovtsev)—we express our sincere thanks and our best wishes on their future research.

There were many kind and helpful people who assisted us during the trip: photographers, artists, translators, drivers, scientists who attended the final symposium, and others who simply came out of the crowd to reveal their experiences and to describe their work. Unfortunately, we were too rushed to be able to acknowledge them individually. But they should know that, even if we were not able to note all their names, we have forgotten neither their kindness nor their hospitality.

The subject of UFOs divides Soviet scientific opinion just as much as it does the Western public. To highlight this controversy, I have presented selected quotes from both sides before every chapter in the text.

During the writing of this book several Western experts helped me in sorting through the mass of material we had brought back from Moscow and to prepare it for publication. Special thanks are due to Larissa Vilenskaya of the Defense Language Institute in Monterey for her gracious help with Russian texts. My agent, Ned Leavitt, provided valuable advice, and Emery Reiff did outstanding work with a manuscript in which complicated spelling, transcribed from the Cyrillic, presented an unusual challenge to word processing.

In that regard, I must confess that, in the interest of readability, I have not followed rigid standards in the transliteration of Russian names. Instead I have tried to simplify them while retaining their most common form of pronunciation, and I have taken the liberty of anglicizing many first names.

—Jacques Vallee
August 1991

CONTENTS

UFO CHRONICLES OF THE SOVIET UNION

A COSMIC SAMIZDAT

CHAPTER 1

THE GLASNOST WAVE

> Some people prefer to remain in a narrow circle of known concepts. They regard anything new as a paradox. It is always the same thing: those people who try to gain new insights into nature are always viewed as an oddity, as a paradox.
>
> *Ernest Chladny,*
> *eighteenth-century Russian pioneer in meteoritics*

This adventure began for me on October 8, 1989, with a phone call from a *Wall Street Journal* editor who knew of my interest in unidentified flying objects. I was working in my study at home in San Francisco, when the phone rang and my friend told me she had just noticed a dispatch that had come across her Teletype.[1]

An editor with the political department of the *Journal*, she was fluent in Russian and conversant with developing events in Gorbachev's Soviet Union. Therefore I paid close attention when she added: "The *New York Times* will be running this tomorrow on the front page. It comes from Tass through the office of the Associated Press in Moscow. It's a landing report from Russia. The sighting happened some time at the end of last month. I thought you should see it right away."

A few minutes later the full page appeared on my facsimile machine. It described some extraordinary events in the Soviet Union, but the wording of the text was even more remarkable.

The Tass dispatch ran this way: "Scientists have confirmed that an unidentified flying object recently landed in the Russian city of Voronezh." (Voronezh is located almost three hundred miles south of Moscow.) "The scientists have also explored the landing site and found traces of aliens who made a short promenade about the park."

The Tass report went on with the assertion that a large shining ball or disk had been seen hovering over the park. Several residents said they watched the UFO land and three creatures, similar to humans, emerge, accompanied by a small robot. "The aliens were ten to thirteen feet tall, but with very small heads," one witness reported. "They walked near the ball or disk and then disappeared inside."

The report also mentioned that a team of scientists, including Professor Genrikh Silanov, of the Geophysical Institute in Voronezh, was studying the case, and that the path followed by the aliens had been ascertained "through the use of biolocation." The people who had seen the aliens "were overwhelmed by a fear which lasted for several days."

THE *NEW YORK TIMES* MISSES A GOOD STORY

Release of the Voronezh sighting data created a remarkable journalistic flap; indeed, sociologists might study it for its implications about the way the public is informed by the most trusted news sources.

By the time the report appeared in the *New York Times* on October 9, the word *biolocation* had been garbled by the prestigious newspaper to *bilocation*, which made no sense whatsoever. The editors had failed to realize that biolocation was a special term in Soviet psychotronic literature that designates dowsing, or *radiesthesia*, the detection of hidden mineral, water, or living entities by paranormal means. Dowsers often use a pendulum, a rod, or a stick for such work.

The Soviets seemed to be saying that they had a team of official scientists studying UFOs using the techniques of parapsychology. That was clearly the real story, yet the American press, led by the *Times*, missed it. Not only did they miss it, but they quickly garbled the few verifiable facts beyond all recognition. They ridiculed the story instead of researching it.

That was only the beginning.

Over the next few days an incredible display of ignorance, confusion, arrogance, and plain stupidity spread over the Western press. The Soviet media, inebriated with the new freedom of glasnost, or openness, did not fare much better. In fact, as American journalists commented with glee, it was as if Moscow had suddenly discovered the joys of tabloids and wal-

Fig. 1. Map of the western part of the Soviet Union.

lowed in their newfound ability to confuse facts with utter fiction.

Instead of investigating and clarifying the original claim, radio and television stations around the world hastily consulted some self-styled experts whose sole expertise consisted of turning the sighting into a joke.

Thus, skeptic Paul Kurtz, Chairman of the Committee for the Scientific Investigation of Claims of the Paranormal, commented that the reports were largely uncorroborated. "In a closed society such as the Soviet Union," he said, shooting from the hip, "you don't get the development of critical reason."[2]

Everybody jumped into the act with cartoons, jokes, and superficial comments. Science fiction writer Ben Bova, president of the National Space Foundation, was quoted as saying he wished the aliens were still there and were holding a press conference.

To conclude its article on the Voronezh affair, the Waterbury, Connecticut, *Republican* was unable to refrain from interviewing a local bartender who claimed "he's served his share of aliens," adding that the beings seen in Voronezh must have come from Naugatuck, where they make their homes. "That's why Naugatuck High used to have such a good basketball team."

On San Francisco radio station KCBS, Kurtz openly mocked what he called the lack of hard evidence, pointing out that two strange rocks reportedly found by the Soviets at the site sounded to him like simple pieces of outer space excrement. In other words, *alien shit*. Another so-called expert pointed out that if such an event had actually happened, President Mikhail Gorbachev would have announced it personally—because it would have been too important to be left to underlings like Professor Silanov! For further comic relief the reporter went on to interview two American cult members from the Aetherius Society, who could be counted on to spew out weird tales about their friendly space brothers.

It was all downhill from there.

Even the psychosociological explanations flourished once more. Some media authorities interpreted the sighting by saying that traditional Russian imagination had always been "wild" and that the UFO story expressed the Soviet people's need for escapism, which had finally blown the lid off the system after long years of repression.

The UFO research community did not conduct itself much better. Someone speaking for the Center for UFO Studies in Chicago, Illinois, stated flatly that his colleagues already knew the answer. "I am certain this is a hoax," the man was quoted as saying in the *Hartford Courant*.[3] He had thousands of "more reliable sightings" in his files that described the space visitors as being three to four feet tall with large heads and spindly bodies. "The reports are remarkably similar down to the smallest of details," he said, to such an extent that the center now uses some little-known details of the aliens' anatomy as a routine test of the validity of the sightings. He implied that the tall occupants described in Voronezh did not fit the center's preordained patterns and the case, accordingly, should be summarily thrown out.

The parade of sloppy reporting and loose thinking continued in the following weeks.

In Howard Blum's book *Out There*, which purported to reveal to the American public the existence of a group of Pentagon intelligence experts secretly studying UFOs, the Voronezh case was mentioned as a topic of hush-hush discussion among CIA and military spooks: a man named Colonel Phillips (who, as it turns out, does *not* exist) was said to be the head of this group of top specialists in the "Great Game" of espionage.[4]

According to Blum, Colonel Phillips suspected that the incident never happened, but he was curious about the identification of the landing site *by bilocation.* Could the Russians be engaged in the same kind of remote viewing studies American psychics have been investigating for many years?

While it is laughable to imagine that a group of professional intelligence experts would leap to such conclusions without bothering to refer to the Russian text (which never used the word *bilocation*) or even without going back to the Associated Press dispatch, we have to consider the very real possibility that American UFO research—including its covert components—has indeed fallen to such a sloppy level. Let us note in passing that American ufology remains nearly unanimous in identifying flying saucers with the idea of space visitors, despite mounting alternative data. Incredibly, even the group of Pentagon technocrats described by Blum never considered any other possibility.

On October 23, 1989, *Newsweek* magazine published an article by Carroll Bogert entitled "They Came from Outer Space—Soviet Editors Discover the Power of Tabloids." Bogert further ridiculed the whole subject, strongly suggesting that the story was a hit with Soviet readers only because they liked to indulge in an age-old fascination with the occult.[5] Tales of flying saucers can be a welcome diversion in times of economic crisis and food shortages, Bogert pointed out. Furthermore, even Soviet newspapers increase their circulation by catering to such weird tales that make people "feel good."

The overwhelming majority of the reports immediately jumped to the conclusion that the aliens, if they did exist, *had* to be from outer space. No other possibility was even discussed. Thus the *San Francisco Chronicle* headline: "Glasnost Makes It Easier for UFOs to Touch Down, Soviets Now Allowing Space Creatures to Land."[6] The article itself was borrowed from the *New York Times* and naturally reprinted the unfortunate error about *bilocation*. No one at the *Chronicle* bothered to check the original Associated Press wire. The article did mysteriously define bilocation as "an extrasensory method of tracking objects or people invisible to the human eye." Supreme gobbledygook.

The story was so sensational that it bounced back to Tass itself, once the most staid and boring institution of all the world's media. Tass seemed to enjoy the renewed attention it received, and it even quoted *New York* magazine media critic Edwin Diamond, who asked: "What did the Academy of Sciences think? Where are the pictures?" It also quoted an American astronomer who said most U.S. academics regarded the story as a joke.[7]

The official consensus of Soviet scientists was not very different. The Academy of Sciences wisely refrained from making any comments, but a Moscow scientist named Vladimir Surdin did go on record with the statement that the Voronezh rumors, like all UFO stories, were "unscientific." Analysis showed that witnesses often mistook jets, balloons, bright planets, or satellites for UFOs. To put it bluntly, when they were not simply airplanes, flying saucers were only as real as rainbows, mirages, or the northern lights. Surdin did not quote a source for such alleged analysis.

While U.S. would-be experts and the true believers reacted flippantly, it became obvious to serious students of the situation that not only the region of Voronezh but a large part of Eastern Europe was in the grips of a major wave that ranked in importance with the largest concentrations of UFO sightings ever reported. Instead of jumping to hasty conclusions, the National Center for Space Research (CNES), the French equivalent of NASA, took the trouble to call Dr. Silanov with a Russian interpreter on the line. Silanov verified the facts and added that a full-scale scientific investigation was in progress in the Soviet Union, with over forty witnesses having already been interviewed. In addition, a literature search turned up a remarkable pattern.

SPHERES, ENTITIES, AND A CURIOUS SYMBOL

Until a large-scale research effort is mounted by our Soviet colleagues, we may not know the true extent of the reports. However, the Soviet wave may well have begun several months prior to September 1989. As early as April 24 of that year an object described as "three times the size of an aircraft" had flown over Cherepovets. That night, at 10:55 P.M., a witness named I. Veselova saw the object hovering a thousand feet in the air.

In the Vologda region of central Russia, on June 6, 1989, schoolchildren near the village of Konantsevo saw a luminous dot in the sky. The dot became larger and soon turned into a shining sphere. It landed in a meadow and moved to the nearby river as the children watched from a quarter mile away. The sphere then appeared to split and "something resembling a headless person in dark garb" appeared, its hands reaching lower than its knees. The sphere and the creature quickly became invisible.

Three more spheres, some of them associated with entities, later landed in the same meadow.

On June 11 at 9:20 P.M. a woman named O. Lubnina saw a fiery ball above Vologda. It was visible for seventeen minutes.

During the summer the newspaper *Socialist Industry*, which does not have a reputation for publishing fanciful stories, told of a close encounter between a milkmaid named Lyubov Medvedev and an alien in the Perm region of central Russia. The alien was a dark figure, taller than a man, with short legs and only a small knob where its head should have been. The figure reportedly became "fluorescent" and disappeared.

In mid-July other Soviet citizens also observed aliens with no heads. And a witness named G. Sharoglazov saw two egg-shaped fluorescent objects as big as airplanes hovering at a height of less than a thousand feet.

Even the Communist party boss of the Chernuschisky region, a man named V. Kopylov, acknowledged that "something unusual is going on over our two collective farms."

Other stories came from the Korovo settlement in the Volga basin. A veterinary surgeon named R. Saitov said he had seen a being over six feet tall, its body covered with dark brown hair. Saitov and a friend tried to approach the creature after spotting it on the far bank of a pond, but it bounded away at astonishing speed. They got into a car in an attempt to chase it but lost sight of it.

Unfortunately, Saratov University's biology department refused to consider the story or even to speak to the witness.

In Shevchenko, on the Mangyshlak peninsula in the Caspian Sea, witnesses saw an object several times larger than a passenger aircraft. It vanished in the clouds above the sea, although its lights remained in sight for a long time. On September 1, residents of Shevchenko saw a "giant cigar" that flew silently over the city and into clouds over the water, its taillights similarly staying visible for a while.

Then came the Voronezh affair that suddenly captured the attention of the world's media.

On the night of October 11, 1989, Soviet television viewers saw a picture of an alleged UFO creature on a news show devoted to the Voronezh landing. It was a figure with two eyes, a nose, and a broad mouth standing inside a glowing, two-legged oval object. When I saw the drawing on French television later that month, I noticed how closely the proportions of the object resembled those of the classic "silvery egg" seen in Socorro, New Mexico in 1964. Like the Socorro object, this one sported an insignia on its side. And the insignia was none other than the UMMO symbol. During the seventies this design had been reported in several cases of close encounters in Spain that turned out to be clever hoaxes by a small cult claiming contact with a space civilization. What was it doing on an egg-shaped craft in a Russian town?

At the time this excitement was bubbling up in the world media, *Le Figaro* had just sent science reporter Martine Castello to California for an analysis of the claims of the New Age movement.[8] I met Martine in San Francisco, and after a quiet dinner with my family and friends, our conversation turned to the Voronezh case. It was during this discussion that Martine and I discovered that we had independently reached similar conclusions about the UFO problem in general and the UMMO controversy in particular.[9,10] Our experience with the inner workings of the scientific community and the media made us suspect that beneath all the ridicule and official denials, some very mysterious and very potent phenomena were indeed being observed in the Soviet Union.

Clearly, we concluded, the time had come to buy some warm clothes and to arrange a trip to Moscow.

Even during the era of glasnost, however, a journey to the USSR is a matter of considerable complexity. Our first inquiries fell on unsympathetic Soviet officials. It turned out, fortunately, that the Soviet press agency Novosti was eager to work with the Western media and especially with *Le Figaro*. Agency officials would welcome our visit. What they could not understand was why we wanted to come to Moscow and limit our interviews to such silly concerns as UFOs. "We have so many more important and interesting scientific accomplishments to show you!" they kept insisting. "We will take you to our cosmonaut training center, the City of the Stars! We will show you our latest developments."

We insisted that UFOs were our highest priority and, skeptical that anything would develop, they reluctantly agreed to forward our request to the various Soviet research organizations they had identified. An unforeseen response took place: the reaction was simply overwhelming. It seemed that dozens of individuals and groups wanted to talk with us. To my surprise, I found that they followed Western research, which circulated in samizdat form, either Xeroxed or partially retyped. Novosti bowed to this mutual interest and helped expedite our visas. And as Paris was still in the midst of the New Year's festivities, we packed our suitcases and looked up the airline schedule for direct flights to Sheremetyevo Airport.

CHAPTER 2

CULTURE SHOCK

> The nature of UFOs is unknown. But whatever they may prove to be—optical phenomena in the atmosphere, probes from other planets, a new phenomenon of nature, or anything else—the study of UFOs should begin with the analysis of the reports.
>
> *Professor Felix Zigel*
> *Moscow, February 1968*

The depression that gradually engulfs you as you get closer to the Soviet Union is not an illusion. Even aboard the Air France jet, with stewardesses in smart uniforms serving champagne and lunch in impeccable style, one could almost touch the thickening gloom. We had entrees over Amsterdam and dessert over Denmark. But conversations became hushed when we passed Riga. By the time we taxied in the grayness of the Moscow afternoon we were all bundled in coats and mufflers, smiles had disappeared, and every passenger was steeling himself or herself for the unavoidable confrontation with surly airport officials, suspicious customs agents, and the uncertainty of everything else.

We stopped with a brief shudder. Suddenly everything was very cold and bleak. It was as if light itself had been confiscated. There was a dreary blanket over the airport buildings, the dusty air, the people themselves. It had snowed and the snow had melted, producing the peculiar black wetness of water mixed with dirt, which is the curse of most northern cities. After five minutes our feet already felt damp. An official, dressed in grayish green, fingered my passport and started asking questions in Russian. I could only shake my head and review in my mind the stern advice I had been given in the West: what to do if they detain you; if they confiscate your passport; if they harass you. Then I recognized my name being called. Suddenly everything was all right. An energetic young man with a smile came forward, shook my hand, and took control. He introduced himself as Genya, an interpreter from Novosti. A few minutes later we were driving toward Moscow.

CAVIAR AND FLYING SAUCERS

"We have prepared a series of meetings for you," said Genya in very fluent French as we drove away from the airport. "Unfortunately, as you know, Andrei Sakharov died just a few days ago. But there are many other people who want to see you."

"Will we be able to meet with the investigators from Voronezh?" I asked him.

"Four of them have promised to come to Moscow to meet with you. They are bringing their maps, charts, and reports. They even have a videotape of their interviews with the witnesses."

The car had traveled through a depressing suburban landscape, and we were now entering the broad network of boulevards in the city itself.

The drive from any airport to city center is often dreary and depressing. I know few uglier sights in all of France than the sewerlike expressway that takes visitors from Charles de Gaulle Airport in Roissy to the northern suburbs of Paris; the landscape one encounters from the JFK facilities to Manhattan always makes me want to turn around and flee, except that there is no place to escape between the various cemeteries and slums one has the privilege of crossing on the way into New York.

The depression that seizes you as you drive to Moscow is of a different sort, however. There are the unavoidable suburbs with all the grayness of their buildings; there are the barracklike housing units lined up like penitentiaries. But I could show you identical gray structures in Saint-Denis and on Long Island, as if city planners the world over, communists and capitalists alike, had hired the same moronic dropouts from the same architectural schools. Yet there is something especially dreary about the drive into Moscow.

The poverty in evidence along the way is not worse than the poverty anyone sees in Paris or New York. What is so oppressive about driving into the heart of Moscow is the absurd evidence of overwhelming bureaucracy, of ever-present red tape. You can see it in the crowds standing in front of the few, poorly lit food stores. You can see it in the eyes of the old women crossing the street in front of the car at a red light. You can see it in the long lines of people shuffling home after work, staring at their feet.

Soon the feeling of gloom was more than we could bear.

"What is happening now in Voronezh?" asked Martine to break the heavy silence hanging over us. "Have more sightings been reported?"

"Oh, yes," Genya answered. "We continue to hear about new cases. But you would make a mistake, if you permit my saying so, by concentrating exclusively on those."

"What interests me about Voronezh is that you seem to have a cluster of many different events in a small area," I pointed out to him.

"But precisely the same thing has happened in many other places. For instance, in the region of Perm in the Ural Mountains, some of my friends have investigated numerous incidents. We even have some remarkable photographs. We've asked one of the local experts to come and meet with you."

"What about Kazantsev?"

"You will meet with him, too. He is inviting you to his home."

"What about Professor Zolotov?" I asked. Alexis Zolotov is legendary for his patient research into the Tunguska catastrophe of 1908.

"He will be here on Tuesday."

"It's going to be a busy week," I told Martine.

The conversation halted. We were approaching the center of the city. Between the big square blocks of the apartment buildings and the centers of administration we could see the lighted towers of old churches and the walls of the Kremlin. The car stopped alongside numerous buses in front of an enormous structure: the Hotel Rossiya (Russia), which would be our home for the duration of our stay.

"Give me your passports and wait here," said our guide.

"I beg your pardon?"

"I must register you with the security office of the hotel. They will return your passports when you leave."

Suddenly we felt trapped again. A man we had barely met an hour before was walking away through the snowy drabness of a Moscow square, taking with him the documents we would need to leave the country, or even to travel beyond city limits. This might be the era of glasnost, noted Martine, but from now on, with our passports safely stored away in the coffers of the police, we would not be able to take a step or talk with anyone without our Russian guides.

Fortunately, the journalists who were assigned to accompany us were far from the stereotype of the burly, surly Russian bureaucrat. They were bright young men with an intense curiosity and a solid sense of humor.

After an agonizingly long delay, Genya came slushing back to the car. We cut through the mixed crowd that clustered around the heavy double glass doors. Genya flashed his identification and we entered the huge lobby of the Russia Hotel.

Like all the hotels reserved for foreigners, the Russia was a huge Stalinesque mass. A thousand rooms were arranged around a central courtyard. The corridors appeared to extend to the left and to the right all the way to the horizon, where you found another set of double doors and another seemingly infinite corridor. At the midpoint of every side of the square, on every level, was a little lobby where a young woman served as watchdog, service supervisor, telephone operator, and concierge. These duties were not as overwhelming as one might suppose, however, because most of the equipment was in such a state of disrepair or antiquity that everyone seemed to have given up on fixing it. I requested a phone communication that first evening, to call my wife in California, but somehow no line to the outside world could be made available until late evening of the following day. An operator eventually came through the next night at 11:00. The old Hollywood expression "Don't call us, we'll call you" must have been invented by a Soviet communications expert. We soon adapted to this sense of cheerful incompetence. After all, our rooms were warm and featured black-and-white television sets with three channels; only one of which, though, had an actual picture accompanied by audible sound. Incredibly, we were being charged a hundred dollars a day for each room.

If it had not been for Genya, we would have starved that night. We went up to one of the large restaurants in the hotel, where another surprise awaited us. Through a mere crack in the massive door a maître d' in impeccable black suit and tie arrogantly asserted that it was utterly impossible to accommodate any more guests. Genya stepped forward and argued forcibly. The man was urged to open the door a little more, and we were able to see that barely half of the room was occupied. Arrangements were quickly made and a waiter preceded us to a table near the window. Once again we experienced the abrupt transition from misery to affluence, from ice to warmth, from hunger to luxury that seemed to characterize life in Russia. Our troubles were forgotten as soon as we sat down. The restaurant overlooked the Church of the Blessed

Basil, resplendent in the glare of a hundred projectors. Our table seemed to be nestled in the sky, with a plunging view of the painted spires and gilded bulbs, and the snow of the square as a backdrop.

It would take us a while to understand why it was almost impossible to be served dinner unless one could pull the appropriate strings, even in such a restaurant where people paid in hard currency.

"In this system, the waiters make as much money if they serve ten guests or if they serve a hundred," someone finally explained to us in a whisper. "And they get to take some of the leftover food at night—to feed their family and friends."

At the next table were eight Russians from the privileged class. They were impeccably dressed, and champagne flowed freely. Did they know that the shops of Moscow were empty, and that scientists and other professionals were spending long hours every day standing in line for a few pounds of potatoes, a fish, or a piece of meat?

The waiter brought us caviar, exquisite salmon, and various specialties. We lifted small glasses of vodka in a toast. There would be many more over the next few days.

"What is so interesting about the sightings around Perm?" we asked Genya.

He described the scene enthusiastically. "The witnesses report some incredible things. Some of our own journalists have seen glowing balls of light drifting eerily through the forest . . ."

"Are there any photographs?"

"Yes, of course. Although the objects are very elusive. But that's not all. They've seen sheets of energy over the fields. And some of the people who did the research have come down with unexplained illnesses."

"With whom is our first appointment tomorrow morning?" I asked Genya.

"You will be meeting Professor Vladimir Azhazha, who heads up the Committee for the Study of Anomalous Phenomena, here in Moscow. He has many things to tell you. And many questions to ask."

Our guide left us after dinner, but we did not feel like sleeping. The urge was too strong to get close to the wonderful structures we had barely glimpsed from the restaurant window, so we sneaked past the guards in the lobby and took our first stroll on Red Square.

LENIN AND THE GIRLS OF GLASNOST

At a time when regimes collapsed, when the Berlin Wall was being chiseled into thousands of chips that were sold off as souvenirs and Christmas gifts, when dictators tumbled, and when the socialist satellites fell from the rigid orbits they had maintained for forty years, it was a thrill to begin the new decade with a walk on the ice that covered the wide square in front of the Kremlin. Over the next five days we would meet the people who had been doing research on paranormal phenomena in the Soviet Union. Some of them would be speaking to a Westerner for the first time, we thought, as we watched the crude white lights on the facade of the GUM department store and the projectors illuminating the crenelated walls of the Kremlin and the Lenin mausoleum. Every minute would be important. We had little time to observe, to understand, to absorb the meaning, the background.

This was a unique period in history. Even the experts were confused.

Hundreds of people were massing around us in the square, waiting for the changing of the guard, always executed with that beautiful mechanical precision that characterizes military operations. But another feeling was clearly detectable, and it was a spiritual current so strong that it rose from the crowd like a song. It had nothing to do with politics, although the sense of a gathering storm must have been in every mind, with the anticipation of a change in the weather of history itself. Among this group assembled from the four corners of the Soviet world arose a fervor that caught us completely by surprise. It was a fervor that bordered on the mystical.

It was a delight to watch the people in the glare of the floodlights. Here again, paradox was the rule. In the West, everyone was well fed, the stores were filled to capacity with meats and delicacies, and the wearing of fur was frowned upon. Here the shops were empty, people were hungry, and the economy was in shambles, but the women strolled across Red Square in full-length mink coats with tall *shapkas* on their proud heads. I briefly caught the eye of one of them: she was a beautiful blonde of thirty or thirty-five. She came toward us like a ship sailing majestically through the frozen Arctic.

"Anna Karenina," whispered Martine.

This was going to be a journey of many contrasts for which we realized we were not adequately prepared. The temperature was three degrees below freezing and falling.

I went up to my room and turned on the television set. The erratic, wavy picture stabilized to reveal a late-evening program of boring art discussion in French about Pope Urban VIII! I could only laugh as I imagined two hundred million Soviet citizens trying to make sense of this absurdity.

The briefing I had received in the United States included some stern recommendations about what not to do in the Soviet Union. "Don't change dollars on the black market. And don't take any men's magazines with you. Pornography is a crime over there. If they find *Playboy* in your suitcase, you'll be in deep trouble."

Thankfully, the program about Urban VIII came to an end. It was followed by an astonishing public announcement by a representative of *Playboy*, who was in Russia to recruit pretty Moscovites who would pose naked for a special issue on "The Girls of Glasnost." Once again, history had overtaken ideology. An enormously vital change was sweeping half the planet, catching all the bureaucracies by surprise: they could take their briefing and shove it! Was the UFO wave of 1989 in the Soviet Union only a symptom, or was it a deep factor in the change? In either case, I now realized, it could not be separated from the historical events that carried it.

CHAPTER 3

RULES OF ENGAGEMENT

During night flights . . . the radar operator discovered clearly defined blips in the 240° to 270° radar sector. They moved on a course of 90° at a speed of 720 kilometers per hour . . . the upper edge of the blips began to come down . . . the lower edge of the blips dropped to the ground. This was reported at another radar station [in the city of Tiraspol] and a request was made that it be checked. The data was confirmed.

Witness N. A. Baydukov, Odeskaya Oblast
April 4, 1966

UFO abductions have become especially common during 1989; so common that we believe we have now identified the mechanism of these events.

Professor Vladimir Azhazha
Moscow, January 1990

Our work started early, with friendly but formal opening remarks by Vladimir Milyutenko, vice-chairman of the Soviet press agency Novosti, who generously placed his office at our disposal for the duration of our stay. We were introduced to his staff and to one of the country's leading UFO experts, Professor Vladimir Azhazha.

"My interest in the problem didn't really start until 1976," said Professor Azhazha, while the pleasant secretaries of Vice-Chairman Milyutenko brought hot tea and sugar on a beautiful tray. "Prior to that I had laughed like everyone else whenever the subject was mentioned. We thought only you, the crazy people in the West, were foolish enough to believe in flying saucers!"

We noted that good-natured, general laughter from all those around the table greeted this statement. That, too, was a new factor.

"What made you change your mind?" asked Martine, who had pulled a pen and notebook from her purse.

All our hosts, including Milyutenko, our interpreters, and various lower officials who seemed to consider it an unusual privilege to witness such an exchange, turned to hear Professor Azhazha's answer. It took all of us by surprise. And it set the stage for the frankness and the extraordinary scope of the revelations that would come in the following days.

ENCOUNTERS AT SEA

"I had to change my mind when I was asked to perform certain hydrospheric studies as a submarine officer in the Soviet navy," Azhazha answered. "After publishing the results of some of our experiments done aboard submarines, I was asked to serve as the scientific director of a group studying underwater UFOs."[11]

Over the years there have been many rumors about similar studies conducted in the United States by the military—studies for which the Air Force's Project Blue Book was only a public relations cover. But results have never been revealed by the Pentagon. The Soviets were obviously taking a very bold step in talking to us so openly.

"What was the year of the study?" I inquired.

"It lasted ten years, from 1976 to 1987," answered Azhazha in a matter-of-fact way that only added to our interest.

I looked around me. The representatives from Novosti were listening to Azhazha's report with a fascination equal to mine.

"Obviously, the Soviet navy has taken the problem very seriously, for many years," remarked Martine.

"We had to. There were too many incidents that could not be denied. It all began when we tried to understand the nature of certain underwater objects that followed our submarines. At times they even anticipated our maneuvers! Initially, we thought they were American devices," added Azhazha, raising a hand to his forehead as he recalled what must have been a difficult research project. "One day such an object came to the surface in a rather spectacular fashion. One of our icebreakers was working its way in the Arctic Ocean when a brilliant spherical craft suddenly broke through the ice and flew up vertically, showering the vessel with fragments of ice. All the sailors on deck and the officers on the bridge saw it. And it was hard to deny the hole in the ice!"

"Could it have been a missile test?"

Our interpreter quickly translated the question and obtained the following answer: "You don't shoot a missile that way. You have to break the ice first. Furthermore, the object was a bright sphere. We knew what nuclear missiles looked like!"

A jovial man with a friendly, round face and a quiet but intensely focused approach to his subject, Azhazha went on with his enumeration of some of the most remarkable UFO cases in the archives of the Soviet navy. "These phenomena were not limited to the Arctic. Our ships in the Pacific also reported flying objects, vertical cylinders. So we ended up drafting actual rules of engagement: what to do when a vessel was confronted with a UFO, how it should be observed . . ."

"How did these objects behave vis-à-vis your ships?" I asked Azhazha, fascinated by his description of these encounters.

"As a superior technology would behave before an inferior one," was the answer. "They treated us the way we would treat a fish, or a rabbit. It is naive to assume they have any goodwill toward us, or any need to interact. They simply seem to go about their business. They coexist with us."

"What was the attitude of the navy hierarchy?"

"Many officers were skeptical, but the reports were hard to deny. They were carefully recorded. On October 7, 1977, a submarine repair ship called the *Volga* was at sea when nine disk-shaped objects circled it. This lasted eighteen minutes. And all the time the radio, the on-board communications systems, all the electronic equipment went berserk. The commander, Captain Tarantin, ordered his men: 'I want you to observe this carefully and to remember it! I want you to take pictures and to draw it, so that when we return to the Soviet Union no one will be able to say that your captain was drunk or crazy!' "

"Were such reports made public?"

Azhazha shook his head no. "At the time, naturally, they were classified top secret. Now we have a more open attitude in this country. We are able to talk about such things. On a few rare occasions I did publish some UFO information, but I paid for it under Leonid Brezhnev. The official reaction was very harsh, very negative. My career suffered as a result, and the directorship of a scientific group was taken away from me."

"What is the situation now?" I asked. "You seem to enjoy much greater freedom."

"We have made a lot of progress. We were allowed to form the Moscow UFO committee. I served as director for the first twelve months, and on July 15, 1988, we organized a countrywide commission, presided by Cosmonaut Pavel Popovich. He is away from Moscow this week. Otherwise he would have been at this table today. Popovich has flown in space twice. Although he never saw any UFOs from orbit, he has observed some unidentified objects as an aircraft pilot."

As Professor Azhazha explained his work, the words of an American skeptic came to my mind. James Oberg, who is frequently featured in *Omni* magazine, had made fun of the Soviet research on UFOs, arguing that it was conducted by "a small coterie of obscure enthusiasts."[12] Shooting from the hip, he had even said of Azhazha that his specialty seemed to be "embellishing foreign UFO reports and fobbing them off as Russian originals." There was only one thing wrong with *Omni*'s sarcasm: none of their writers, least of them Oberg, had ever taken the trouble to meet Azhazha.

This wasn't an informal conversation with some drunken journalist in a Berlin coffee shop or with a marginal visionary at an international New Age congregation; this was Moscow. The paneled walls of the Novosti executive offices were gleaming with a well-polished look. On the desk were books, files, and a calendar from Aeroflot. Staff people took notes, drank tea, and periodically put out their cigarettes in glass ashtrays. Sometimes our exchanges were halted by animated arguments in Russian that our interpreters were hard-pressed to follow. What we were hearing had never been said in the West. Some of it had never been said publicly in the Soviet Union. But one thing was already clear: the Russian researchers of the UFO phenomenon had enough real data of their own not to waste their time fobbing off Western sightings, as the flippant remark by James Oberg suggested.

RUSSIAN ORIGINALS

Over the next two hours the former submarine officer described for us the wide panorama of the Soviet UFO archives, including many cases he had personally studied.

"I know you have argued that UFO phenomena are as old as mankind itself," Azhazha said to me. "Well, we have documents from the Middle Ages that mention similar unidentified objects. You would also be amused to read such reports in Russian newspapers from the period 1910 to 1912."

"Have you found a random time distribution among Soviet cases, or do they occur in waves, as they do in the West?" I asked.

"They definitely occur in waves. We have recorded

three major ones. The first one occurred in 1966–67, the second one between 1977 and 1979. But it was poorly documented because no specialized service was in existence at the time. On the contrary, the latest wave of 1989, which seems to continue as we speak, has given us a wealth of data—up to fifteen cases per day. In a single incident, which took place on October 5, 1989, in Kirov, there were between 100 and 120 objects."

"Can you describe some of the specific features of last year's wave?"

"There were many large cylinders, horizontal cylinders," answered Azhazha as he consulted his notes. "For instance, less than a year ago, on February 13, 1989, between 9:00 and 10:00 P.M., such a cylinder flew over a road at an altitude of less than one mile. This happened in the Transcaucasus, in Cabardino-Balcari. It seemed to be metallic, and its length was estimated at about 1,500 feet. Its nose was lower than its tail, and it flew at 65 mph."

I prompted him to continue. "Were there several witnesses?"

"Actually, it was seen by thousands of people—truck drivers, people in cars. It seemed to have spotlights in front and in back. And some porthole-like openings were visible along its sides. It flew over the city of Nalchik, then drifted down to an altitude of 150 feet, made a turn, and flew off.

"The most interesting fact about this case is that, as the object turned, people saw some fins on its tail. But when the turn was completed, the fins had vanished. We have other cases where parts of the objects seem to materialize on the spot."

Azhazha bent toward us across the table for emphasis. "This is a key characteristic of the phenomenon: it is polymorphous."

Unsure that I was getting an accurate French translation of that last sentence, I asked Azhazha to repeat what he had just said.

"These objects are polymorphous. They can change shapes dynamically in flight."

I took a document from my briefcase. It was a reprint of an article I had written: "Five Arguments Against the Extraterrestrial Origin of UFOs." In that article I had mentioned the ability of the objects to materialize on the spot and to change shapes as a fact pointing toward a multidimensional origin rather than a simple spatial or interplanetary origin for the phenomenon.[13]

Azhazha read the section of the article I was presenting to him. Then he looked at me in surprise, put down the papers, and said: "We have reached very similar conclusions. It is as if you and I had been working together for the last ten years."

HUMANOIDS AND PSYCHIC PHENOMENA

"As investigators, we are only one element of a system that links together the object, the percipient, and the space around them," continued Azhazha. "Therefore we must consider the psychophysical interaction that may take place between the object, the witness, and the noosphere—the plane of human consciousness. If we don't consider such interaction, the sightings make no sense at all."

"Can you give us an example?"

He thought about my question for a moment, then

went on: "Last year in Vologda some spheres were seen in the sky. They were about sixteen feet in diameter. What was unusual was that these spheres did not look like a craft at all. Instead they resembled a woman's face. This seems absurd. What can we do about such a report? We do not even have a good working hypothesis. Yet the logic of the events shows that the phenomenon has existed as long as human civilization itself, as we said a moment ago."

"How do you deal with humanoid reports?"

Azhazha had obviously expected that I would ask him this question. He sipped some tea, sat back in his chair, and said calmly: "We have many reports of such beings. They vary widely in their appearance and size, from some nine inches to forty-five feet in a report from the Volga region in 1989. I hasten to say that we have not yet analyzed this case, so I will not vouch for its reliability; it is simply too recent."

"How do you approach this problem?"

"The first challenge we face is to try and detect the real signal in the midst of a great deal of noise. We find that the witnesses are generally sane. What is obvious is they have healthy minds, contrary to what many academic scientists think. But the observations are truly bewildering. When a UFO being appeared in Vologda it seemed to be flat, and its head was lower than its shoulders! People who saw it from the side reported it seemed to be only about three inches thick. Such reports obviously challenge everything we know, unless you are right with your theory about other dimensions being involved, beyond ordinary space-time."

I consulted my notes before addressing him again. "I have read reports about some of the witnesses themselves actually disappearing during the sightings in Voronezh. Can you confirm this?"

"Yes. This took place on September 27. Some of the observers vanished and later reappeared. The same phenomenon was reported in Vologda. A woman from the village was walking along in her bathrobe without realizing that a UFO entity was nearby. She just seemed to be attracted outside by something. The witnesses screamed to catch her attention, but she didn't hear them and she just kept walking. When she came close to where the being was, they both vanished on the spot. About half an hour later she reappeared, yelling in fear. Our colleagues in Leningrad are trying to locate her again. In such cases we always work through local teams."

"It would seem that it would be simple to find her, in a small village . . ."

"It's harder than you think. This was a simple woman who is very much afraid now. She has gone into hiding. The other witnesses are scared. People are traumatized. All we know is that she could not remember anything when she reappeared."

ABDUCTION PHENOMENA IN THE SOVIET UNION

I pressed on, my curiosity in a feeding frenzy. "This last case you mentioned, the woman from the village, is what we refer to in the West as an abduction. Are such cases frequently observed in your country, and have you been able to find any particular pattern?"

This was the question I had been itching to ask all morning, of course. Almost nothing was known about abduction cases outside the Anglo-Saxon literature.

"Abductions have become especially common during 1989," Azhazha said, "so common that we believe we have now identified the mechanism of these events. I will give you three examples."

Our pens were flying as we took notes over the next hour.

The first case mentioned by Azhazha took place in a suburb of Nicolayev at midnight on September 16, 1989. Nicolayev is a city of a half million people, a Black Sea port about seventy miles northeast of Odessa. A young woman who worked at the meat-packing plant there had left her job early to catch the tramway home. She was alone. The tramway lights came into view. Suddenly she realized she was being levitated to a height of 160 feet. In the meantime the whole crew had left the plant and saw their coworker floating in the air, alongside an unidentified object.

"Naturally, everyone started yelling and screaming," Azhazha told us, "and eventually she was returned to the ground. But we wonder if many isolated people are not abducted this way."

The second incident occurred near Nalchik, in the Caucasus, on October 11, 1989. A sixteen-year-old girl who was in a courtyard was approached by an object. She was not abducted, but she suffered severe burns on her hands and had to be hospitalized for stress. The actual location was the village of Maelski, and the time was between 6:00 and 6:15 P.M. The girl, Natasha Barinova, was a student at a technical college and was well regarded by her teachers. She had walked home and had reached the yard in front of her house when she felt that she was being lifted up, as in the case in Nicolayev three weeks earlier. But the unusual aspect in this particular event is that she saw a net falling toward her from the sky. In the center of the net was a bright white point. She tried to push it back and received an electric shock. When she screamed her voice came out sharp and shrill, as if acoustic waves had been distorted by the atmosphere around her. Her family rushed out of the house and saw her in the air, with a flying disk hovering less than fifty feet away.

"What was the nature of her injuries?" I asked Azhazha.

"It was as if something had tried to pull the skin from her fingers. The tips of her fingers were enlarged."

"How did the event end?"

"The disk vanished and she found herself back on the ground. She was paralyzed for a while."

The most remarkable case, an abduction attempt, took place on July 4, 1989, in a park near Kiev, on the shores of the Dnieper River.

It was twilight, but there was enough light to see clearly. Two women, Vera Prokofiyevna, a retired employee of a factory in Darnitsa, and her friend Alexandra Stepanovna, an engineer, together with Alexandra's six-year-old daughter, were strolling in the park. The following is the story told by Prokofiyevna.

The party came closer to the river and suddenly saw a "boat" and three beings on board. The beings looked very pale and had absolutely identical faces, like identical twins. They had long blond hair, big eyes, and were wearing collarless silver shirts that looked like nightgowns. The beings bluntly told the women that they came from another planet: "Our planet is so far that your mind cannot fathom that. When you become like us, you will know. Every day we take one person from Earth to our world. We will take you. Our ship is nearby; we will show it to you." They spoke Russian with a strange accent that Prokofiyevna called "ancient," rather than foreign.

The transcript does not say how the beings left the boat and started walking along with the women. "One walked in front of us, and two with us," Prokofiyevna reported, "one on each side, as if they were guarding us. I wanted to shout and run, but I was drawn to them as if by a magnet and I had no strength. When they looked at me, I felt like needles were all over my body. Alexandra Stepanovna became very pale; I believe I looked no better. We started begging them not to take us, because we had families and children.

"Behind some trees, we saw a craft. It was silvery, like their clothing, and looked like a huge barrel with a circular antenna on the top of it."

The little girl became very scared and started crying. The two women also reacted with deep anguish. "Well, we won't take you," they were told. "We will find others." They went inside the "barrel" by using a ladder with three steps. The ladder moved by itself inside, the door closed by itself, like an elevator, and the craft took off without any noise, without causing any wind, and without disturbing the sand beneath it. Soon it turned into a small star.

The incident was investigated by Alexander F. Pugach, who holds a Ph.D. in physics and mathematics and is a research fellow of the Department of Physics of Stars and Galaxies of the Ukrainian SSR Academy of Sciences Observatory. Dr. Pugach was familiar with Western research of UFOs and with descriptions of contactee experiences. He believed the sighting to be genuine, judging from several small details: the device took off without disturbing the sand; the boat was without sails, oars, or engine; the beings did not show any emotions. He argued that no physical apparatus landed in the park and later took off. He thought, however, that this was a real phenomenon and that the women were not lying, but that the nature of the phenomenon was more complex. In his opinion, one could not exclude that some force, some beings, might have projected the scene into the minds of the women. In other words, his position is close to the views of those, like myself, who believe that UFOs are from a different dimension or another reality—although in my opinion, this does not exclude a material, physical presence at the time of the sighting.

"This particular abduction mechanism we categorize as *Dialego*, the dialogue, because it usually begins with a verbal exchange," Azhazha told us.

"But this last case is almost like a fairy tale," I pointed out. "We cannot study this subject as a purely technical problem."

"I agree with you," answered Azhazha. "Ufology is a complex domain that demands knowledge of biotechnology, of space physics, and of psychology and sociology. We need a multidisciplinary approach. Historians and folklore experts should get involved. We need psychics and we need physicists. We even need philosophers."

The representatives from Novosti looked at their watches and indicated that it was time for lunch. We could continue our conversation at the cafeteria, they said, and in the afternoon we would meet with the investigators who were coming from Voronezh.

CHAPTER 4

THE VORONEZH COLLECTIVE

Suddenly a light appeared, not very bright, trembling and flickering. The beam came down and it slowly moved along the ground toward us. It seemed strange that the surface touched by the ray was full of bluish sparkles, and everything was quivering as if one was in a haze on a hot day. . . . When the beam approached the car I experienced an unpleasant feeling of fear and loss of self-confidence.

Voronezh witness M. N. Polyakov
September 1989

On September 27, at about 7:00 P.M., I was walking in the area of the park. Suddenly I noticed a luminous ball sweeping past on a northerly course at an extraordinary speed, strictly horizontally at an altitude of roughly six hundred feet. I estimated its diameter to be about forty-five feet. . . .

Lieutenant Sergei Malveyev
Voronezh Militia

Four members of the Voronezh collective, a regional investigation group, were waiting for us when we returned from lunch. They were typical Soviet engineers, businesslike and practical. After the formal introductions they told us that they belonged to an autonomous UFO group formed under the auspices of the Radio-Engineering, Electronics, and Communications Society, the Soviet equivalent of the American Institute of Electronic and Electrical Engineers. The group included Alexander Mosolov, an aviation engineer; Vyacheslav Martynov, chief engineer at an aeronautical plant; and Dr. Yuri Lozovtsev, who held a Ph.D. in engineering and was a specialist in materials science. The fourth man was a journalist from the Voronezh television station, who recorded a short interview with us. I found it ironic that Martine and I, who had come all the way to the Soviet Union to understand the local wave of sightings, would end up being interviewed for the benefit of the people of Voronezh.

Soon the television interview was over, the cameras were put away, and we got down to business.

WHAT HAPPENED AT VORONEZH

As we review the events that took place in that region, it is important to remember that Voronezh is not a small village but a large city of nearly a million inhabitants. Founded as a fortress in the late sixteenth century, today it is an industrial center for machinery, electrical products, chemicals, cigarettes, and processed foods.

The first report of the UFO incident in Voronezh appeared in the local newspaper *Kommuna.*[14] Written by A. Mosolov and entitled "A Soccer Game with Aliens," the article told about the object seen on September 27, 1989, at about 6:30 in the evening, while schoolchildren Vasya Surin and Genya Blinov played soccer in South Park. But they were not the only witnesses. A girl named Julia Sholokhova and approximately forty adults observed the strange occurrence. That was one of the facts missed by the Western media, who kept talking derisively about "a UFO seen by a bunch of kids."

The witnesses related that they first saw a pink or red light in the sky, which turned into a dark red sphere, about thirty feet in diameter. The object was circling forty feet above the ground, and witnesses could see that the grass under it was affected. Soon the sphere flew away.

A few minutes later the UFO returned and hovered above the park. By then the adults had joined the teenagers. Everyone saw a hatch open in the bottom section of the sphere. A being appeared. It was nearly ten feet tall and was wearing silver-colored overalls and bronze-colored boots. The being seemed to have three eyes and a sort of disk-shaped object on its chest. It appeared to scan the terrain, then closed the hatch. The sphere came lower. As it did, it brushed against a poplar tree, which was bent and stayed in that position.

The UFO, which measured about forty-five feet by nineteen feet, landed. The being emerged, accompanied by an entity that looked like a robot. The alien uttered something and a luminous rectangle, about two and a half feet by four feet, appeared on the ground. The alien said something else and the luminous rectangle disappeared. The alien adjusted something on the robot's chest, causing it to walk in a mechanical way.

It was at this moment that one of the boys cried

out in fear. The alien simply looked at him and the boy instantly froze, unable to move. The eyes of the alien seemed to be emitting light. Everyone started shouting. Somehow the sphere and the beings vanished on the spot.

Five minutes later the sphere and the three-eyed being appeared again, just as strangely as they had disappeared. The being now had at his side a tube about four feet in length. A sixteen-year-old boy was close to the scene. The alien pointed his "rifle" toward the teenager, and the boy instantly disappeared. The alien entered the sphere and the sphere flew away, gradually increasing its speed. At the same instant the vanished teenager reappeared.

The story, as reported in the article, ended with two statements: (1) that the above was written after interviewing multiple eyewitnesses and (2) that Voronezh residents had observed UFOs not once, but many times over the period of September 23 to 29.

On October 7, 1989, *Kommuna* continued a discussion of local observations of UFOs in an article entitled "What Was It?"[15] The story was written by O. Donin, a reporter for the newspaper, who mentioned statements made by two adults: Yuri Vokhrimenko had seen a red sphere in the sky from his balcony on September 27 at approximately the same time as the teenagers in the park; another witness named B. G. Yatsunov, a former pilot, had also seen a UFO on September 29 at 8:10 P.M.

The rest of the article consisted of an interview with Professor Genrikh Silanov, a physicist from the Spectral Analysis Laboratory of the Voronezh Geophysical Institute and a member of the Section on the Study of Anomalous Phenomena of the Society for Radio-

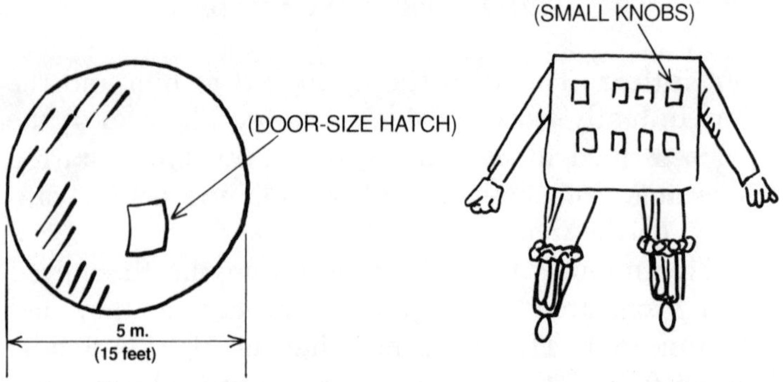

Fig. 2. Drawing of the Voronezh object and of the robot occupant seen by Roma Torshin, a sixth grader. Note the absence of any symbol or insignia.

Engineering, Electronics, and Communication. He related that at least three landings of UFOs had taken place in Voronezh. The earliest one had been observed on September 21 at 8:30 P.M. by boys from Mendeleyev Street. A sphere had landed, and two humanoids and a robot had emerged from it.

According to Silanov, the investigators had been able to trace the outlines of one of the landing sites through the use of biolocation techniques; it was a circle sixty feet in diameter. Within this circle a dowsing rod gave a "definite response," he said. Investigators also used a device developed by Silanov to measure the bioenergy of humans. They found that inside the circle the bioenergy level was nil. Silanov reported that this effect had been observed previously at several UFO landing sites.

Within the circle investigators later found four depressions in the ground, each about two inches deep and six inches in diameter. The depressions were located at the four points of a diamond-shaped geometric figure. Again, by using biolocation, Silanov claimed that he reconstructed the actual path of the humanoids who took several steps away from the craft. The path later shown by the boys who had seen the beings was exactly the same, he said, although they were not aware of the biolocation findings.

In an interview with the Soviet national daily *Izvestia*, Vladimir Azhazha summarized the observations in Voronezh and wisely added, "I personally believe that it would be a mistake to interpret these facts as evidence of visits by extraterrestrial aliens; our knowledge is still too limited for any convincing scientific interpretation."[16]

THE INVESTIGATIONS BEGIN

On October 11, 1989, the newspaper *Selskaya Zhizn* published an interesting article in which S. Plotnikov summarized his interviews of the eyewitnesses in Voronezh over the period September 21 to October 7 and named the primary observers. The article noted that among those who saw a red sphere about thirty-five feet in diameter, at an altitude of a thousand feet, were economist V. A. Agibalova and her daughter, Tatiana; an employee of the local power station, I. V. Nikitina; a retired woman, Y. T. Illarionova; a graduate student of the Veronezh Engineering Construction Institute, I. Alexseichev; and the chief engineer of the Design Institute, Y. N. Sviridov. All these people observed the object on various days, between 6:00 and 9:00 P.M.[17]

Clearly, the idea of a few teenagers fantasizing

about giants in the park had to be eliminated. Another Western media fact was biting the dust of reality.

V. A. Kugatov, a specialist in geodesics from the Agricultural Research Institute, observed a UFO on September 24 at approximately 10:30 A.M. That particular UFO resembled a giant airship and was flying very fast. It moved first to the east and then to the west.

The article also provided additional details about the schoolchildren who made the initial reports. On September 21, the landing was observed by seventh-grade students (approximately thirteen years old) A. Lukin, Y. Levchenko, and S. Borisenko. Eleven-year-old Vasya Surin, who saw the landing on September 27, was in the fifth grade and his friend Genya Blinov, in the sixth. The author related Silanov's observations of the site and added that, in addition to four depressions, holes in the ground had been found, "as if someone had taken a soil sample."

In a local Voronezh newspaper, *Molodoy Kommunar*, journalist Eugene Buslayev interviewed Alexander Mosolov and Vyacheslav Martynov.[18] They described the field studies that used dowsing. They also related another interesting detail: when they used a magnetometer and attempted to measure the intensity of the magnetic field at the landing site, the intensity turned out to be so high that it was beyond the scale of the device. Their colleague, Dr. Yuri Lozovtsev, calculated the pressure on the ground from the shape and dimensions of the depressions and came up with the figure of eleven tons, assuming it was caused by static pressure, that is, by the actual weight of the apparatus. That weight is in the range of estimates reached by French scientists who have studied physical traces from UFO landings at sites like Quarouble and Trans-en-Provence.

THREE TYPES OF UFO ENTITIES

The Soviet researchers also related that eyewitnesses of four landings described not one but three different kinds of beings who had emerged from the various UFOs seen at Voronezh. The first kind consisted of ten-foot-tall beings with three eyes. Two of the eyes were whitish; the third, in the middle, was red and devoid of a pupil. The second kind was a robot, actually a box with something resembling a head on the top of it. In one of the observations no head was seen. Instead there were two antennae on the top of the box.

In a typical observation, a hatch in the sphere opened, a small metal ladder appeared from the hatch, and two tall beings brought a robot out from the sphere. The robot had knobs on its chest. A tall being touched some of the knobs, and the robot began walking in a mechanical way. In ten to twenty minutes the robot returned to the three-eyed beings, who turned it off and carried it back into the sphere. The ladder then automatically went inside, the hatch closed, and the UFO rose from the ground. Almost instantaneously it became a mere dot and disappeared in the sky.

Readers of my book *Confrontations* may recall a very similar case that took place in Venado Tuerto, Argentina. In that sighting a boy named Oscar, whom my wife, Janine, and I personally interviewed at the

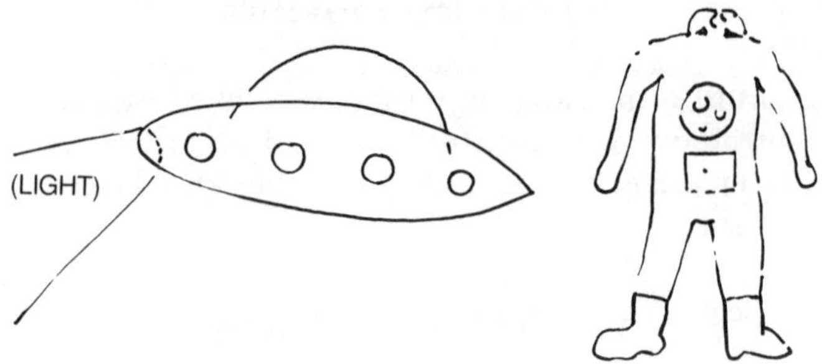

Fig. 3. Drawing of the Voronezh object and of the being seen by Genya Blinov, who observed "two eyes and slightly above them a red lamp." Note that no insignia was reported on the object.

site of the encounter, saw a landed craft with a "giant" and a robot companion.

The third kind of beings seen at Voronezh were small, with grayish-green faces and blue overcoats that looked like loose raincoats. They had two eyes.

Another Soviet paper, *Meditsinskaya Gazeta*, sent reporter Valery Milyutin to Voronezh. He interviewed several adult eyewitnesses who saw the UFOs, adding many useful details.[19]

Thus Yuri Petrovich Vokhrimenko gave the following statement:

> On September 27, between 6:00 and 7:00 P.M., I saw from my balcony a reddish sphere appearing over the horizon. It flew at a relatively low altitude toward the left bank of the river, hovering over the village of Otrozhka, and then it disappeared behind the houses. It was not moving fast. It flew at the speed of a small plane.

Valentina Alexeyevna Agibalova, a senior economist at the State Bank Computer Center, and her daughter, Tatiana, a deputy prosecutor of the Zheleznodorozhny District in Voronezh, stated:

> On September 27, around 7:00 P.M., we saw a red-colored sphere flying from Shilovsky forest toward the Voronezh hydroelectric power station. It hovered over the left riverbank and then vanished. [The Russian word literally describes a light going out.] Then it reappeared and moved back toward the forest.

Inna Vladimirovna Nikitina, an employee of Voronezh-Energo, the local power station, said:

> Around 9:00 P.M., for five to ten minutes, I observed a fairly large flattened sphere, shaped like an orange. This happened in the vicinity of the mining equipment plant. I experienced a feeling of intense fear for which I could not account.

Yuli Nikanorovich Sviridov, chief engineer of the Trans-Electro-Project Design Institute stated:

> Around 8:00 P.M., on September 27, from the fourth floor balcony, I saw a big, bright red sphere move between the houses at an altitude of a thousand feet, with a crimson halo along the edges. Its speed was comparable to that of a small plane. It was moving from the left bank of the river in a westerly direction.

What we have here is a case of highly qualified multiple witnesses to a series of physical events for which there is no current scientific explanation.

THE CASE OF THE PARALYZING RAY

Another witness, M. N. Polyakov, a factory worker, reported one of the most remarkable episodes in the whole series. His statement runs this way:

> At the end of September we were driving to the southern suburb of Voronezh. All of a sudden our headlights went out. The radio died out in the middle of a song. The engine died, too. The car coasted, giving us a chance to get on the shoulder of the road. We tried to turn the ignition key back and forth in vain. The driver wanted to have a smoke, but the car lighter did not work. He took out some matches, but they would not ignite. The driver threw away his cigarette in frustration and he went out to take a look under the hood. And then I heard his voice, with a tone of intense surprise: "Look, look, quick!"
>
> He stood there with his arm outstretched, pointing toward the sky behind the car. I turned around and saw a pinkish-yellow sphere shining dimly above the road about three hundred feet away. It was hard to tell its size because of the distance, but I am certain that its diameter was over thirty feet. At the bottom of the sphere there was a protuberance that reminded me of a ball-shaped growth on a tree. Suddenly a light appeared from it, not very bright, trembling and flickering. The beam came down and slowly moved along the ground toward us. It seemed strange that the surface touched by the ray was full of bluish sparkles, and everything was quivering as if we were in a haze on a hot day. Once in a while there was a blinding flash that was reflected by the surface. When the beam approached the car I experienced an unpleasant fear. I felt constrained. I did not want to move or to

do anything. My good mood disappeared without a trace.

The ray moved over to the car hood. The engine started to smoke the way it does when the radiator is overheated. There was a feeling of something slipping in. The car moved and something appeared on the driver's seat. I sensed an alien presence; I felt that I could stretch my arm and touch the invisible being. And although my brain and my willpower ordered my hand to touch the unpleasant thing, I could not move my arm. What was it? Fear? Was I like a rabbit hypnotized by a cobra?

Then the ray moved away. Then I could breathe easier. For several seconds it was dark and quiet, and then, great! The dashboard lit up! The radio came back on as if nothing had happened. The driver turned on the engine.

Now everything was back to normal. My fingers were tingling as they do during a cramp. The driver was silent, but I was dying of curiosity. "What could all this mean?" I asked him.

"What are you talking about?"

"About the ball."

"What ball?"

"The one above us, when we stopped."

"Did we stop?" He seemed surprised.

Now it was my turn to be surprised. Maybe I should go to a doctor, I thought. Maybe I am a little tired? Or maybe I just fell asleep? We approached the streetcar stop. I got on, and when I reached for the handle there was a powerful spark between my fingers and the metal. I felt a strong and unpleasant electric shock.

I came home and when I put the key into the keyhole I got another powerful shock. All night long I had unusual dreams. I woke up with a headache. And then exactly at noon I suddenly felt fine.

> I am fifty-six years old and nothing unusual has ever happened to me. I am almost perfectly healthy, and I had no intention of telling that story to the press: people might think that I am a lunatic. But my friends convinced me.

The author of the article, Valery Milyutin, concluded with the opinion of O. V. Stolyarov, department head at the newspaper *Kommuna*, who has studied such anomalous phenomena for several years:

> The celebrated Russian scientist Konstantin Tsiolkovsky admitted the possibility that space and time were multidimensional. Moreover, he thought that ethereal beings could live in a parallel dimension to ours. Why don't we see them? Perhaps one of the most convincing answers has been offered by one of the leading authorities on this issue, an Academician of the Siberian Branch of the USSR Academy of Medical Sciences, Vlail P. Kaznacheyev. He is convinced that ancient people were capable of sensing one another at huge distances. Then this ability was lost by most people. Maybe that is why some people see humanoid beings and others do not.

We spent the rest of the afternoon discussing the reality of the observations at Voronezh. We probed, we argued, we debated. As the next chapter shows, our conversations with the Voronezh collective only deepened the sense of mystery attached to the sightings.

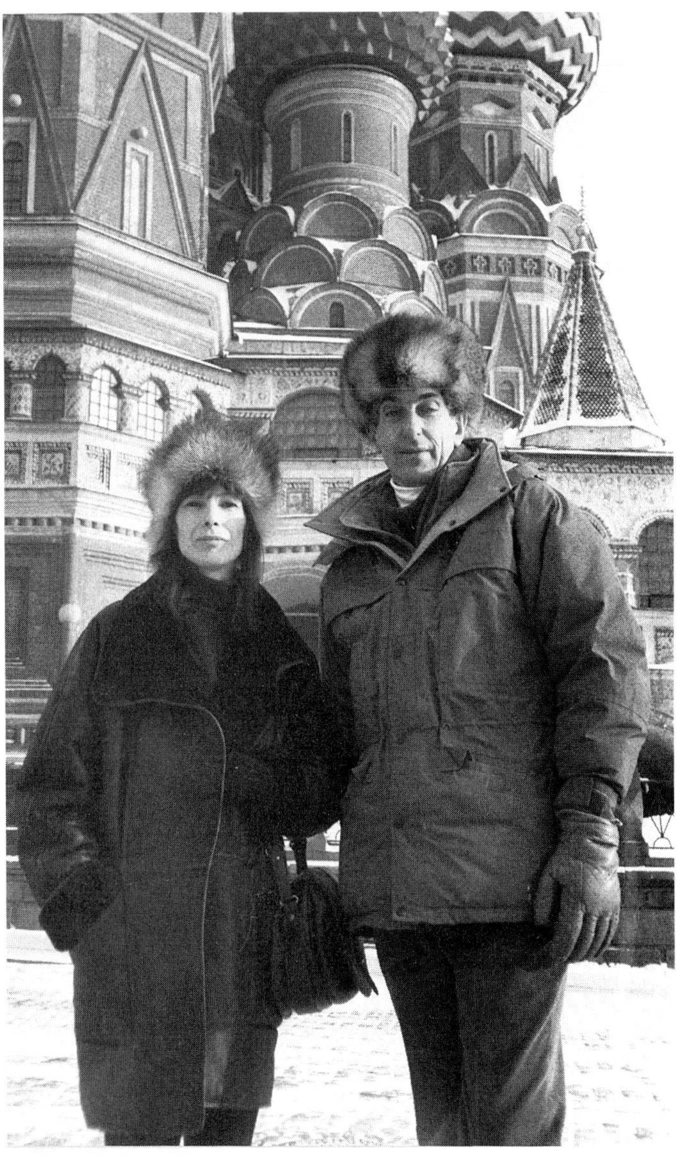

Martine Castello and Jacques Vallee in Moscow in January 1990.

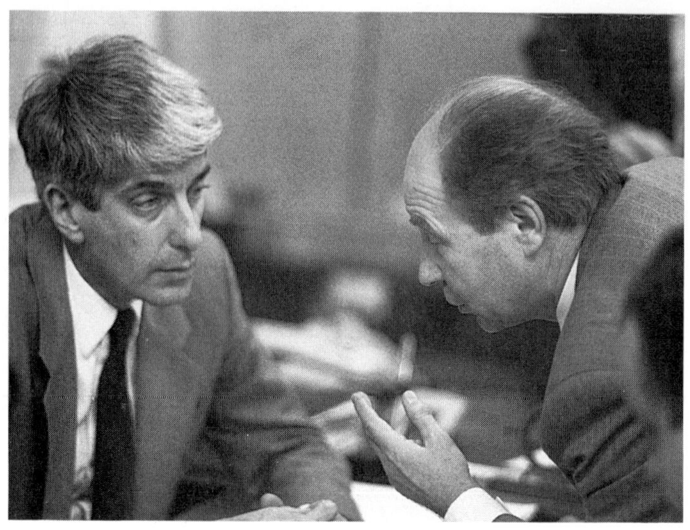

Jacques Vallee in conversation with Vladimir Azhazha.

This painting of a close encounter during the 1989 wave in the Soviet Union is part of the Cosmos exhibit in Moscow. The attempted abduction happened near Kiev, on July 4, 1989.

Meeting with the Voronezh collective.

Arguing about the use of biolocation techniques at Voronezh.

Artist's rendition of the Voronezh landing based on reports by witnesses. Note the UMMO symbol on the belts of the alleged aliens.

A portrait of the writer Alexander Kazantsev.

Porphyry Ivanov, the founder of a Soviet UFO contact cult.

Some of Ivanov's followers practice bathing in icy waters and walking naked through the snow while they wait for the next contact with extraterrestrials.

At Novosti, debating UFO phenomena. Alexei Konin, the young journalist standing at right, was a witness of unexplained objects in the Perm region.

A luminous object seen in a clearing during the 1989 Russian wave. The face of the humanoid "occupant" was also described as emitting light.

During a research trip to the Perm region in the middle of winter a member of Novosti took this photograph of a globe of light in close proximity to another member of the expedition, who actually saw the object.

A group of investigators in a clearing in the Urals, with unexplained light phenomena evolving around them.

A luminous object flies over the forest in the Perm region.

This photograph was given to me by a Russian journalist as "evidence" of unexplained energy fields near Perm. It is obviously a short time exposure of a beautiful but perfectly ordinary auroral display. Any amateur astronomer would recognize the Big Dipper in the sky, showing that the camera was pointing north. The length of the star trails establishes the duration of the exposure. But why were we told that there was anything unusual about this photograph? Perhaps we were being tested.

The Moscow symposium of January 12, 1990.

CHAPTER 5

THE VORONEZH INVESTIGATIONS

Over thirty people have witnessed the landings in Voronezh. Thousands have seen the objects in flight.

Aviation Engineer Alexander Mosolov

I don't know what actually happened here, but an increase in the radioactive background is in evidence. What is the reason?

Colonel Lyudmila Makarova,
head of the Criminal Expertise Department,
Voronezh Internal Affairs

"The center of the activity varies within the city of Voronezh itself," Alexander Mosolov told us after we had reviewed the background of the various cases. "It moves from the park to the power plant. Many of the sightings seem to occur in polluted areas. The park itself used to be a garbage dump. It was covered over with dirt and planted. Similarly, the electrical plant and the site of the future nuclear plant have been visited." With a trace of frustration in his voice he added: "We do not know what all that means."

"How did you first hear about the case?" we asked the group.

Mosolov was the first to answer. "You see, I live in the part of town where the children had the first close encounter," he said. "One of the kids' mothers told me about it, and I went to the site the very next day. But we found out that the sightings in the area had actually begun back in August. Over thirty people have witnessed the landings in Voronezh. Thousands have seen the objects in flight."

"And the wave isn't over yet," pointed out Vyacheslav Martynov.

QUESTIONS OF METHODOLOGY

"What was your methodology in the Voronezh case?"

"We began with the schoolchildren," answered Mosolov. "We separated them. We found out that many of them did not know the others. We had them make separate drawings, and we videotaped them while they were being interviewed. We will show you the tape later."

"What did they actually draw?" asked Martine. I knew that, like me, she was anxious to find out if the symbols reported by the kids were genuine.

The men from Voronezh had brought some of the original drawings and paintings. They started spreading them on the table before us.

"They drew classical shapes, as you can see. A sphere or a disk, resting on four legs. And indeed we found four imprints in the ground," pointed out Dr. Yuri Lozovtsev.

"The humanoids are similar in all the drawings," added Martynov. "They have no neck, their head rests

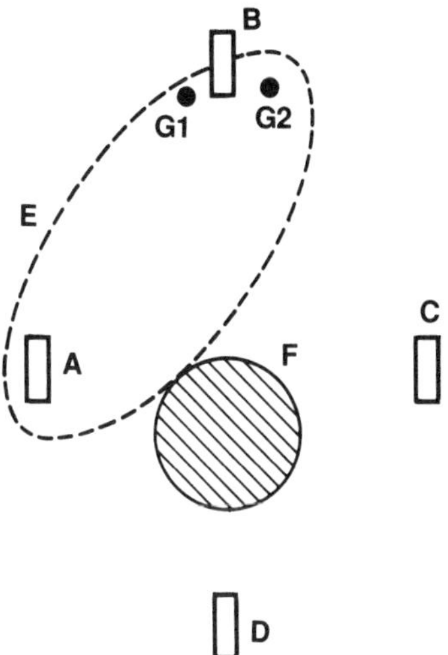

Fig. 4. Diagram of traces found in the first Voronezh landing in South Park:
A, B, C, D: rectangular imprints

E: area of flattened grass
F: epicenter, radioactivity level double that of the background
G1, G2: holes fifteen inches deep, vertical and smooth

on their shoulders. They look like a target at a firing range."

"What about the eyes? Is it true that the witnesses described three eyes?"

"Some of them did, but others saw *two* eyes and something else on the forehead, which could have been a device of some sort."

"Tell us more about the physical traces in South Park," I insisted. The group was eager to comply. After all, they were all technicians, trained in hard science. In that respect we were speaking the same language.

"We measured the intensity of the magnetic field

and the parameters of ground magnetism. We found the traces of the craft's four legs, which were an inch and a half deep. And we took many soil samples for analysis."

"Was there any evidence of a rise in temperature?" I asked, thinking of the Trans-en-Provence case where French government scientists had found evidence of heating to 600° Celsius.

"No," was the answer. "But the soil had turned to the consistency of stone, and there was an area of flattened grass."

"We computed the total weight of the object," added Lozovtsev. "As we mentioned before, we found eleven tons, which is consistent with some of the estimates you have given in your work from French encounters. Of course, this is only an approximation. The object may not have rested on the ground with its full weight."

Martynov chipped in with more astonishing data. "The background radiation was in the range of ten to fifteen microroentgen per hour, while the measurements taken on the trace itself were between thirty and thirty-seven. Although it doesn't pose a threat to people's health, such an increase is clearly significant."

"Can you trust the children's testimony?" I asked.

Lozovtsev was quick to reply. "It is hard to deny the initial sightings, since there were physical traces and also adult witnesses. But in the following days there were other reports from children and we do *not* trust those reports. For example, the press stated that a sixteen-year-old boy had suddenly seen an object appear close to a tree . . . that may have been an invention."

"What about the sightings by adults?"

"Those are not in doubt. There were simply too many witnesses, and we have their statements on record. For instance, there is a case where the first witness, a mother of ten, was getting everything ready for a family celebration when she saw something flying over adjacent buildings. Soon there was a crowd of five hundred other witnesses. The object was seen for two and a half hours! It was a dark disk with three blinking lights: red, yellow, and green."

"Did any of the cases involve a beam of light, other than Polyakov's experience?"

"Yes. Near a lake called Vor's Sea several women saw a beam coming from above. It hit the water and continued inside the lake. They were not caught in the beam, but they suffered strong headaches nonetheless."

"There were other cases of high strangeness," continued Mosolov. "One of them involved a lens-shaped discoid object, about twenty feet in diameter, that took off from a platform that seemed to be set on wheels . . . I have spoken with the witness myself. The platform simply vanished on the spot. I would have had trouble believing this, except that a round trace was left in the grass, with the vegetation bent in a spiral as if a giant comb had been run through it."

Now the conversation became general.

"There were also some reports of direct contact," Martynov said. "The most recent one took place less than a week ago, last Wednesday. A forty-year-old woman who was in her house with her son saw a pinkish-colored light behind the window. Next she described three dark silhouettes that had neither eyes nor ears. They seemed to be calling her. We found that this woman was in good mental and physical health. Until that sighting she had always refused to believe in UFOs. The experience lasted an hour, and during all that time she couldn't move from her bed."

Evidently the Voronezh group had been serious, thorough, and diligent in its work. But a number of problems still had no solutions.

UNRESOLVED QUESTIONS

"There are two aspects of the case that we do not understand," I said after exchanging a quick glance with Martine. "The first has to do with the use of biolocation to study the site, and the second has to do with the symbol that the witnesses have drawn on their representations of the craft."

Again, everyone jumped into the conversation, so that the interpreters had trouble following what was said. We did gather that Professor Genrikh Silanov had performed the dowsing studies.

"Silanov has a long experience with this technique and with magnetism generally," said the researchers. "He used it in Siberia when he was on mineral resources search trips, looking for metals."

Mosolov drew a rough map of the area. Over the next half hour he proceeded to explain to me the nature and the amplitude of the "magnetic signal" Silanov had found in the vicinity of the traces. I must admit that this was one of the most confusing aspects of our conversations with the Soviet investigators. I had the impression that the parameters they were using were undefined and that the phenomena they were supposedly measuring were poorly calibrated. If there was an effect, I asked, how could they be sure that it was related to the presence of an object, rather than a more mundane cause, like underground water flow, or a metallic mass? After all, the park had been built over a landfill that used to be a garbage dump. How did they know what it was they were measuring?

"We had better show you the videotape," they said. So we went down the hall to one of the modern television studios maintained by Novosti, a room filled from floor to ceiling with the latest Japanese video technology. A moment later we were watching Professor Silanov walking up and down the grassy area where the sighting had taken place, carefully holding in his hand a bent, L-shaped metal rod, with the longer part of the rod pointing ahead of him. Periodically it would deviate to the left or to the right, a fact that was duly measured and noted.

We also heard and watched the witnesses of the first landing being interviewed. They seemed to be very articulate, and showed no reluctance to describe what they had seen.

Yet when we came back into the office to review the case one more time, I continued to have trouble with the Russian concept of biolocation. From their point of view it seemed as obvious as measuring electrical tension with a voltmeter. From my point of view, I failed to see any calibration, any reliable baseline to their measurements. Obviously, I was missing something: I could not see how they could relate the movement of the rod to the possible presence or absence of a UFO in that park several days earlier. I still don't. From a Western scientist's point of view, much of the Soviet UFO data is poorly documented and often surrounded by irrelevant facts. But perhaps serious Soviet researchers have the same impression of the American UFO scene, where sloppy hypnosis of abduction victims and garbled reports of crashed humanoids are often mixed in with the verified reports in the literature.

We gave up on the biolocation argument and began discussing the symbol some of the witnesses had drawn on the side of the UFO. Not only did it appear on the object, but it was also on the belts of the aliens who were seen next to it. Martine cornered the representatives from Voronezh and told them about her own extensive investigations into the UMMO cult in the West.

"That symbol is genuine," said a member of the group. "It was first reported in our region in a case that dates from 1984."

There was disagreement on this point among the researchers in the room. A similar symbol had been reported on May 22, 1979, by a Polish citizen named Woldemar R., who saw it on a strange object that landed in a park near Warsaw. When Martine pointed out that the insignia had first been associated with a Spanish episode that was widely regarded as an outright hoax, Boris Churinov, from an investigation team calling itself the Twenty-First Century Group, said that years before he had published a report on UFO shapes that included the UMMO insignia. That report had long been available in Voronezh, he added. Could it be that one of the witnesses had remembered it and had added the insignia to his drawing in a misplaced effort to increase its credibility?

If that were the intent, certainly the opposite result had been obtained. On the basis of that drawing, some of my scientist friends in France had rejected the whole Voronezh affair, hinting darkly that perhaps Soviet intelligence agencies were behind those alleged messages from UMMO as well.

It was a quarrel we did not resolve that day. We came away convinced that a genuine series of extraordinary phenomena had taken place in Voronezh. We believed that the UMMO symbol was a spurious addition, the result of unfortunate contamination induced by overenthusiastic believers. And on the topic of biolocation we found ourselves as confused as ever. Perhaps our conversations the next day with Professor Zolotov, of the Geophysical Institute in Kalinin and an expert in magnetism, would clarify the situation.

CHAPTER 6

TUNGUSKA: THE CONTINUING ENIGMA

Tonight the sky is covered with a dense layer of clouds. It is still pouring rain, and yet it is extraordinarily light. In fact, it is so light that outdoors one can read small newspaper type fairly easily. There should be no moon, but the clouds are illuminated by a sort of yellowish-green light that sometimes turns to pink. . . .

Academician A. A. Polkanov
Siberia, June 1908

It is very difficult to sweep aside the explanation that the Tungus catastrophe was an atomic explosion. The inquiring mind is anxious for scientists to produce the true explanation.

Alexander Kazantsev
A Visitor From Outer Space, *1966*

When we got up the next day, the little corner place at the end of the long hallway at our hotel had run out of instant coffee, so we had a quick breakfast of tea and dry bread. Conversation was not about paranormal phenomena but about worsening economic conditions, the failure of perestroika, and Gorbachev's future at the head of an empire that seemed torn apart by centrifugal force. The weather, too, was getting harsher, and we bundled up in scarves and fur hats for the drive to Novosti.

"I can talk to you about four different topics," said Professor Alexis Zolotov, who was waiting for us in Milyutenko's beautiful office, which was fast becoming our shelter from the cold and dampness of Moscow. "We can discuss the Tunguska disaster, we can discuss biolocation, or we can turn to the subject of biological fields or of unidentified flying objects in general." He favored us with a genial smile.

"Let's begin with Tunguska," I said in response to this gracious opening. "I have read your works on the subject."[20]

"You mean my earlier works. You are probably not aware of the latest developments."

Over the next three hours we discussed Zolotov's study of the extraordinary explosion that rocked Siberia in 1908.

JUNE 30, 1908: THE EVIDENCE

Believers and skeptics alike agree that the major frustration in the study of UFOs comes from our inability to establish firmly the physical facts. Even in a remarkable situation like the Voronezh case, when we have actual traces, multiple witnesses, and repeated events, it is very hard to come away with the proof that a truly paranormal event happened. One may be personally certain that it did, but the kind of evidence that could convince the scientific world to sit up and take notice simply does not yet exist.

It is this feature that places the Tunguska case in a class by itself. No scientist could deny the reality of the phenomenon. The only disagreement could be on the various hypotheses created to explain it.

Everyone also agrees on the date and the exact time: June 30, 1908, at 7:00 A.M.

The reasons for such an exceptional consensus in a field known for its controversies and endless polemics are very simple. Alexis Zolotov, who had personally traveled to the site in 1959 and 1960, summarized them for us, his sharp eyes darting from Martine to our interpreter and then to me, his hands smoothing his long gray beard. "It began with a blinding ball of light, brighter than the sun, that appeared over the Siberian taiga near Vanovara. It turned into a fiery column rising up into the cloudless sky. Next, a loud explosion reverberated several times. The sound was heard as far as 750 miles away. The earth moved and even at that distance chandeliers swung from the ceilings. Four hundred miles away a train nearly derailed under the shock. The engineer actually stopped his engine, wondering what had happened. Some men who were riding as far as 200 miles away were thrown from their horses. Windows that faced toward the explosion were shattered in houses 150 miles away. Roofs were torn off and fences were uprooted at a distance of sixty miles or so. Earth tremors were recorded in Irkutsk, Tashkent, as well as Jena, Germany. The shock wave, recorded by a seismograph in London, circled the globe twice. Luminescent clouds were observed and even photographed over Europe and North Africa. Newspapers could be read at night by the light of the clouds. So you can see it was hard for the skeptics to deny that something had happened."

Pointing to a detailed map in a copy of his book on the Tunguska catastrophe, Zolotov continued his de-

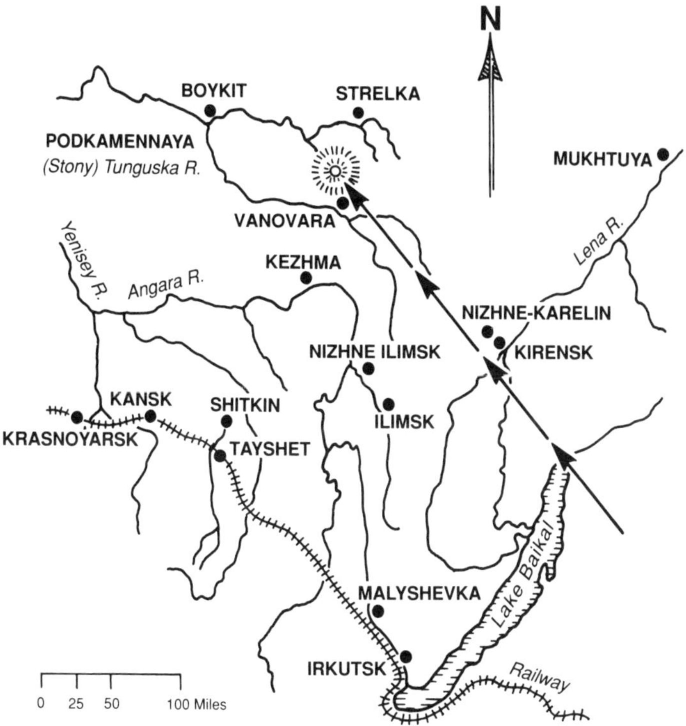

Fig. 5. A map of the region where the unexplained Tunguska catastrophe took place in June 1908.

scription. "Within sixteen miles of the site all the trees were uprooted. Within ten miles they were burned by luminous radiation. And what do you think took place at the very center of all that unprecedented destruction? *Nothing!* Nothing at all. There was no crater, and the trees themselves were left standing."

"Is there a hypothesis to account for these effects?" asked Martine.

Zolotov seemed to think this question was very funny. His eyes sparkled and he leaned back in his armchair as he replied. "Of course there is! You know how we scientists are. Not one, or a dozen, but over a hundred hypotheses! Unfortunately, very few of these theoreticians bothered to go to the spot and see for themselves. Everybody got into the act. Meteors, comets, asteroids—it seems every phenomenon known to man has been twisted in one way or another to try and fit the facts. But everything failed. Modern science still provides no satisfactory explanation."

I had to agree with Zolotov's comment. None of the English-language books I had read on the matter provided a logical, rational solution to the mystery.[21] The best explanation in favor among scientists is the cometary impact hypothesis, but it remains unproven.

NO TRACE OF IMPACT

"The crux of the whole problem, the real secret, is that the explosion took place at an altitude of three miles . . ."

"How do you know that?" Martine broke in. "I mean, if there is no trace of impact . . ."

"Precisely. Don't forget that the uprooted trees, thousands of them, provide a perfect map of the catastrophe. They all pointed away from a central site. Yet at the epicenter itself nothing had been destroyed. The force of the explosion blew downward from the object, along a cone, not horizontally at all as it would have in a collision."

Taking a piece of paper, Zolotov began drawing a rough sketch for us. "If a foreign body had actually hit the earth at a speed of about three miles per second, over 10,000 miles per hour, there would have been a sudden heating of the soil which could have risen to thousands of degrees and a crater of up to sixty miles would have been formed. You have a perfect example of that with Meteor Crater in Arizona. But where is the Tunguska crater? It does not exist. Nothing actually hit the ground there."

Flipping the pages of his book to a map of the devastated area, he went on. "As you can see from the pattern of the fallen trees, the force of the explosion does not decrease equally in all directions away from the epicenter. The destruction created a heart-shaped wave with two clearly separated lobes."

"Was anything actually found at the site?" I inquired.

"Nothing, and that's the real paradox. If it had been a meteorite, the mass at the time of impact would have had to be in the range of a thousand tons, still assuming a speed of three miles per second. There would obviously be a crater. Many fragments of the object would be in all the world's greatest museums. Instead we found nothing at all."

"Is there any way to establish the exact speed?"

"We only have an approximation. The velocity must be in the range of three to eighteen miles per second. The object arrived from the southwest, traveling in a northeasterly direction. Clearly speed is the key question. What we observe is destruction caused by the conversion of kinetic energy, which is measured by mass multiplied by the square of the speed, into light and thermal energy."

"It must be possible to estimate that total energy from the pattern of destruction," I said.

"Oh, yes, we have done that," said Zolotov, quickly

paging through his book to show us the formulas he had developed.

"The total energy, measured in ergs, was the number 10 followed by twenty-four zeroes, which is equivalent to a forty-megaton nuclear blast."

THE TUNGUSKA INVESTIGATIONS

A witness named S. B. Semenov, a farmer living forty miles away from the site of the Siberian explosion, described the effects in the following way:

> I was sitting on my porch facing north when suddenly, to the northwest, there appeared a great flash of light. There was so much heat that . . . my shirt was almost burned off my back. I saw a huge fireball that covered an enormous part of the sky. . . . Afterward it became dark and at the same time I felt an explosion that threw me several feet from the porch. I lost consciousness.

Another witness said that after the fire that destroyed the forest, local people who went out in search of a reindeer herd found only charred carcasses.

Yet the cataclysm aroused no scientific curiosity for thirteen years. True, everyone had assumed that the object was a large meteorite, which was not exciting enough for an expedition to be mounted. The region itself was reputed to be almost inaccessible. It is an area of rolling taiga, huge swamps, and primeval forest. The mosquitoes are ferocious and the winters are so severe that birds have been known to drop frozen from the air.

It was only in March 1927 that mineralogist Leonid Kulik and an assistant set out from Tayshet with supplies and equipment to locate the site of what they assumed was a large impact crater. Maps were inaccurate and the high latitude confused the compass, but Kulik eventually reached Vanovara, where he was able to question eyewitnesses. In mid-April, suffering from scurvy and other diseases, the two scientists saw the astonishing effects of the devastation. But when they finally reached what must have been the epicenter, they found themselves in a standing forest. There was no sign of a meteorite.

Kulik's sensational report to the Academy of Sciences triggered a second expedition in April 1928, during which Kulik and others conducted a magnetic survey, still hoping to find fragments of an object.

The following year a better-equipped expedition camped at the site for eighteen months, obstinately digging in every depression in the expectation that sooner or later they would unearth the huge meteorite that must lie there.

It was in the early 1930s that the comet hypothesis was first proposed. It was independently suggested by F. J. W. Whipple of Kew Observatory in London and by I. S. Astapovich of the Soviet Union. A gaseous comet would have left no trace of its impact after its nucleus exploded in the atmosphere with a kinetic energy level of 10^{21} ergs per second. "It was this explosion that gave rise to the seismic and air waves," said Astapovich, "while the high-temperature explosive wave caused the uniform scorching."

The problem with this theory is that more recent estimates of the energy released place it at 10^{23} ergs per second, a hundred times greater than proposed by the two astronomers. Zolotov's figure, as we saw, is actually still ten times higher.

As unsatisfactory as it may be, the comet theory still represents the most common explanation given in science books today. But Zolotov disagrees with it.

Zolotov himself led expeditions to Siberia in 1959 and in 1960. He noted an alterance of burned and unburned zones that Professor Felix Zigel of the Moscow Aviation Institute interpreted as evidence of luminous radiation, some areas being shaded from direct exposure to the light.

Further evidence of radiation damage was provided by the observed diseases of the reindeer and by genetic changes in the plants in the area of the impact, with a significant increase in cell production. Radioactive cesium 137 was found in abnormal quantities in the 1908 tree rings.

Soviet authorities and U.S. experts such as physicist Willard F. Libby estimated the energy yield at thirty megatons, 1,500 times greater than the Hiroshima atomic bomb blast. At Hiroshima wood was ignited only to a distance of one mile and the range of the destruction was a mere eighteen square miles, Alexis Zolotov reminded us, putting into perspective the enormous destruction he had witnessed in the taiga.

THE COMET THEORY

"So it could not have been a meteorite," said Martine. "This brings us back to the possibility that the object was a comet, as Carl Sagan and others have argued."

Personally, I must confess that I have always found the comet theory hard to follow. There were numerous professional and amateur astronomers scanning the sky for such objects every night at the turn of the century. Comets that come close to the earth are easy to spot and to track. They develop tails that are illuminated by the sun, and their trajectories can be plotted with precision. So how could a cometary body hit our planet without warning? It might have come directly from the direction of the sun, of course, so that it would be masked by daylight. In recent years, there has been increased awareness that such cometary nuclei might go undetected and hit the earth in large numbers, but the theory is controversial. Furthermore, Zolotov argues that both the mass and the velocity would be too small to explain the devastation recorded in Siberia. Shouldn't we find many traces of such objects, just as we find evidence of meteorites? And what caused the explosion itself, if the object did not hit the ground?

"We don't see how the speed of the comet at the time of impact could have exceeded a few miles per second, and that is insufficient to provide the energy figures. Remember that meteorites crash at speeds of up to twenty-five miles per second. Furthermore, the comet would have left tell-tale traces, metals, minerals, even if it was primarily composed of ice, which would have melted away. We are beginning to know a lot about the composition of comets. The space probe *Vega* has recently approached Halley's comet and measured its density. None of this supports the idea that the Tunguska explosion was due to a comet's nucleus. Sagan's theory is fine, except that it isn't supported by the facts."

"Where does that leave us, then? What is your current conclusion?" I asked.

"It was a nuclear blast," said Zolotov. "It was caused either by an artificial body or by a phenomenon that is still eluding our researchers."

"What about a black hole?"

"There should have been two catastrophes if it was a black hole: one for the entrance and one for the exit. Yet we have only one explosion."

"Well, one catastrophe is enough for me," joked Martine as Zolotov and our interpreters joined in the laughter.

"Some Russian writers, notably Alexander Kazantsev, have argued that the explosion could be due to antimatter," I went on.[22]

"We had to eliminate this theory, too," said Zolotov. "The explosion would have taken place at a much higher altitude, as soon as the antimatter came into contact with the stratosphere."

"How do you explain the heart-shaped pattern of destruction on the ground?"

"There must have been interaction between two waves. That is the only explanation I see. The ballistic wave was combined with another source of energy. I tend to believe the speed of the incoming object was indeed quite low, only a few miles per second, and the explosion was not caused by conversion of kinetic energy alone, but also by release of internal energy, like a nuclear bomb."

"What did the eyewitnesses say about the object's trajectory?"

"Some people saw it move from west to east, but it seemed to reverse its course just before impact."

"That seems to suggest a purposeful maneuver," I pointed out, remembering that Professor Zigel had used this argument in his lectures.

"True. But the observation of a change in trajectory, by itself, does not prove it was an artificial object," concluded Zolotov. "Every year we make a little progress in documenting the phenomenon, but we still don't have any explanation for it. We are just as puzzled today as we were before."

This puzzlement, apparently, was not shared by the Japanese specialists who traveled to the site in 1989. Stating that their research clearly indicated that the catastrophe had been due to a nuclear-powered spacecraft, they erected a monument at the site, the first such memorial commemorating an alleged UFO crash.

CHAPTER 7

FOR THE RECORD: A BRIEF HISTORY OF SOVIET UFOLOGY

In the city of Petropavlovsk, at approximately 11:00 P.M., with comrades Perekhov, Negayev and Yevmenenko, I observed two very strange disks which moved one behind the other and then changed formation and moved as a pair. Passing almost directly above us they emitted light toward the ground. When we fell into the zone of illumination I felt something oppressive.

Air Force Reserve Officer S. N. Popov
March 1964

Enough has been said and there are no grounds for the revival of these absurd rumors that were buried many years ago.

Academician Y. A. Artsimovich
Quoted in Pravda, *January 8, 1961*

While many UFO buffs are often selective in their references, citing only the most recent or the most sensational research (or even that small part of it that happens to agree with their own pet theory), Soviet intellectuals are like most European scholars. They insist on giving credit where credit is due and they place a high degree of importance on the accurate history of the phenomena they study. Therefore, certain names of pioneers recur throughout conversations and the samizdat literature. At this point in our narrative it is useful to pause and provide the reader with a wider perspective on UFO research in the Soviet Union.

Whether they agree with them or not, Soviet ufologists acknowledge the influence of three great founding fathers—namely, the late Yuri Fomin; Professor Felix Zigel, who died of a heart attack in November 1988; and Alexander Kazantsev, a popular science fiction writer born in 1906, who is still very active in the field.

Professor Zigel is the best known of these men in the West because he served on the faculty of the Moscow Aviation Institute.[23] A respected scientist, he was a cofounder (with Kazantsev) of the short-lived Stoliarov committee formed in 1967 at a time when the University of Colorado was starting its own ill-fated study of UFO phenomena in the United States. Headed up by nuclear physicist Edward Condon, the Colorado group was funded by the U.S. Air Force. It quickly degenerated into an unscientific, biased whitewash and led to the closing down of official UFO investigation in the United States.

Without allowing himself to be discouraged by the lack of official sanction for his research, Zigel compiled (among other works) a courageous book in February 1968. Entitled *Unidentified Flying Objects in the Union of Soviet Socialist Republics*, this volume of 165 pages was the first to make available the details of numerous reports from the entire country. What the book didn't say was that the road to the compilation of Zigel's study had been a long and arduous one.

THE PIONEERS

If we set aside the extraordinary Tunguska event we briefly reviewed in Chapter 6, the first *modern* UFO sightings were recorded in the Soviet Union in May 1946, over a year before private pilot Kenneth Arnold first spoke of seeing "flying saucers." The observations included landings, thus giving the lie to a theory that is still popular among amateurs in the United States, arguing that landings are typical of a "later phase" of the phenomenon.

According to the journalists Henry Gris and William Dick, who traveled through the Soviet Union in search of paranormal stories in 1972, Yuri Fomin, who had studied these early files, was convinced that telepathic communication was taking place between human witnesses and UFOs. Many close encounter observers had "heard a voice" inside their head that said things like "do not be afraid, we mean no harm to you," he reported.[24]

Yuri A. Fomin was a professional engineer, a senior instructor for the automation department of the Moscow Technological Institute. He had begun in 1956 to collect information on UFO sightings throughout the Soviet Union. With two other engineers, B. V. Makarov and V. M. Gulisov, Fomin issued reports and gave public lectures about the phenomenon. It seemed that an open attitude on the problem would prevail, until a venomous article appeared in the January 8, 1961, issue of *Pravda*. Entitled "The Truth About Flying Saucers," it quoted the skeptical comments by a prominent academician, Y. A. Artsimovich, who in turn cited Harvard astronomer Donald Menzel as the authority on the nonexistence of the problem and attacked ufologists as "completely irresponsible persons."

As a result of this exercise in character assassination, Yuri Fomin's membership in the All-Union Society for the Propagation of Knowledge was terminated. As Felix Zigel put it, "The study of UFOs stopped for many years in the Soviet Union."

Gris and Dick met Felix Zigel in the early seventies at the home of Alexander Kazantsev. They described him as a balding man, his body bent forward under an invisible weight, with a sad look in his eyes. At the meeting they discussed the hypothesis that UFOs might be visitors from a planet thought to have existed between the orbits of Mars and Jupiter, where the asteroid belt is located. The Soviets called the missing planet Phaeton. But Zigel was very open-minded and considered many other possibilities.

Prior to the late sixties, researchers like Zigel had kept a prudent silence in the Soviet Union. Not only were their jobs threatened by the "rationalistic" attitude of the all-powerful (and all-skeptical) Academy of Sciences, but the central government was very paranoid when it came to UFO reports.

During the cold war the Kremlin regarded such observations as a psychological warfare ploy masterminded by the Pentagon and the Central Intelligence Agency. Soviet officials thought that such "hysterical" rumors were deliberately planted to create unhealthy agitation and fear among socialist countries, taking the workers' attention away from productive pursuits.

UFOs IN THE SOVIET UNION: HISTORICAL DATES

June 30, 1908	Tunguska catastrophe
May 1946	Numerous sightings including landings
1946	Kazantsev suggests that the Tunguska object was a spaceship

(1947–1956: FIRST DARK PERIOD)

1956	Yuri Fomin begins study of Soviet UFO files
1959–1960	Fomin, Makarov, and Gulisov give lectures
January 8, 1961	*Pravda* quotes Artsimovich and Menzel. Calls ufologists "irresponsible." Fomin forced to stop research
1962	Menzel's book translated into Russian

(1961–1966: SECOND DARK PERIOD)

August 1966	International Mathematics Congress in Moscow
1966	Zolotov's expedition to Tunguska
August 24, 1967	First pro-UFO Kazantsev-Vallee article in *Trud* sells 22 million copies
October 18, 1967	Stoliarov committee formed
February 1968	Zigel publishes book on Soviet UFOs
February 27, 1968	*Pravda* quotes Moustel, Martinov, Lechkutsov: "No UFO ever recorded over the USSR!" Stoliarov committee disbanded

(1968–1988: THIRD DARK PERIOD)

1970–1988	Zigel, Azhazha pursue work underground: some public lectures, a few articles, but no publicity
1988	Zigel dies
Spring 1989	"Glasnost" wave begins
September 1989	Voronezh sightings attract worldwide attention

The only Western book on the subject to be translated and published in the Soviet Union was Donald Menzel's *Flying Saucers* (1962). Oddly enough, it has now come to light that the late Professor Menzel himself had enjoyed a long association with the U.S. intelligence establishment.

Two researchers who have done a special study of UFOs in socialist countries, Ion Hobana and Julien Weverbergh, credit me with helping encourage Felix Zigel to "go public" in the late sixties.[25] In the summer of 1966, I attended the International Mathematics Congress in Moscow. On that occasion I was able to bring to the Soviet Union some up-to-date news from the West, as well as direct information about the research Dr. J. Allen Hynek and I were pursuing, some of which has never been published to this day. According to Hobana and Weverbergh, this contact encouraged Zigel and a few others to take a public stand on the issue of UFOs.

When Tass announced in 1967 that a radio astronomer named Cholomitsky had observed a source located in the constellation Pegasus that seemed to emit intelligent signals, the news stimulated the Soviet ufologists to act. On October 18 of that year an official committee for the study of the phenomenon was formally organized.

THE STOLIAROV COMMITTEE

Under the presidency of Major General Porfiri A. Stoliarov, with Zigel and Kazantsev as vice-presidents and engineer Arkadi Tikhonov as secretary, the committee received the enthusiastic support of four hundred scientists, cosmonauts, and engineers. Soon Zigel and Stoliarov were publicly discussing UFOs, emphasizing facts and verified sightings over theories and fantasy.

The world press reacted quickly to the new Soviet attitude. Sensational articles by Henry Kamm[26] and by Walter Sullivan in the *New York Times* stressed the similarities between the Condon committee and the Stoliarov group. While the Condon study was financed by an official Air Force contract, however, the Stoliarov team was purely a private volunteer effort, which was highly vulnerable to the sanction of higher authorities. Brandishing the *New York Times*, a Russian debunker, the astronomer Y. A. Artsimovich, rushed before the Soviet Academy of Sciences, demanding immediate sanctions. Vladimir Lechkutsov, the secretary of the National Committee of Soviet Physicists, stated loudly that there was no official organization for the study of the UFO phenomenon in the Soviet Union. That was a severe blow to the Stoliarov committee. On February 27, 1968, an article published in the authoritative *Pravda* proved to be the final assault. Signed by E. Moustel, the president of the astronomy council of the Academy of Sciences, and by D. Martinov and Lechkutsov, the article flatly asserted that no unidentified flying object had ever been recorded over the Soviet Union, an utterly ludicrous statement. For good measure Moustel and associates invited Donald Menzel to repeat his arguments for the Soviet public. The Harvard scientist obliged in the January 1968 issue of *Vokroug Svieta*. Soviet ufology went underground again.

To this very brief summary of the early period of UFO research in the Soviet Union could be added many interesting comments, but the time has not yet come to make them public. It should be clear, at the very least, that we do not have the whole story. Recent revelations about the close, even intimate relationship that existed between Dr. Donald Menzel and American intelligence agencies—a relationship of which the Soviet Union must have been aware—suggest that the Academy of Sciences may have had important reasons to scuttle the naive Stoliarov effort. Certainly, if top scientists in Moscow already knew that the Condon report was designed to reach a negative conclusion on the existence of the UFO phenomenon, they were justified in avoiding a public relations debacle by dropping out of the game as early as they could. A *New York Times* article by Walter Sullivan establishing a parallel between the two committees may have scared them, not because they didn't want to study UFOs, but because they already knew that the University of Colorado study was only a farce perpetrated on the American scientific community. If so, the Soviets were either very smart or very well informed: indeed, the Colorado study was destined to end in disgrace.

Soviet authorities had another reason not to welcome an open investigation of their own alleged UFO sightings. Contrary to what the public was told, there were many confirmed UFO sightings throughout the Soviet Union. A colleague who traveled to Moscow in 1968 brought word to me of the real reasons for the demise of the Stoliarov committee when he came to Paris later that year. Arkadi Tikhonov wanted me to know that the Soviet military had gathered not just a few but many thousands of unexplained cases. It was the overabundance of data, not the lack of such, that triggered the end of the open scientific study.

THE MODERN PERIOD

As Martine and I found out during our meetings with Vladimir Azhazha and with other researchers, work had indeed been pursued in the USSR in spite of the official denial. Some of it was the result of continuing private interest. Courageous individuals like Zigel and Kazantsev were not easily intimidated. Furthermore, they had earned high honors as Soviet citizens (Zigel even held the prestigious Order of Lenin, and Kazantsev is a much-decorated veteran who was awarded the Order of the Red Star for his services as the head engineer of an army complex) and could not be completely silenced.

Other studies proceeded quietly, as we now recognize, under the auspices of the military. Some of them took place outside the Soviet borders. For instance, when a reservist from the Cuban army had a close encounter with a UFO in June 1968, Fidel Castro's experts called on Soviet intelligence specialists to conduct a very thorough investigation of the whole affair. (Perhaps they had forgotten to read the academicians' explanation of UFO phenomena in *Pravda* the previous February?)

The case deserves to be quoted in detail because it illustrates the richness of the Soviet UFO files and the fact that these files are obviously not limited to the Soviet Union itself, just as American files actually cover the whole world.

The individual involved in the encounter, Isidro Puentes Ventura, was forty-two years old and lived close to the village of Cabanas. His file in the army reserve described him as a serious man who was responsible and could be trusted. On June 14, 1968, he was ordered to stand guard in an area of the countryside he knew well. His duties began at 6:30 P.M. and ended at 2:45 A.M., when he was supposed to turn in his weapon and sign the roster.

Five minutes past midnight several machine-gun rounds were heard, coming from Puentes's location. Several patrols went out to look for him. They found him at dawn, unconscious. He was transported to the provincial hospital in Pinar del Rio where he remained in shock, unable to speak for six days. He was moved to the neurological ward at the Naval Hospital of Havana, where the leading experts who studied him found no brain damage and diagnosed strong emotional trauma. He remained in shock another seven days.

In the meantime, Cuban intelligence had taken over the site and contacted the Soviets. Investigators found forty-eight spent machine-gun casings and fourteen bullets flattened by impact against some extremely hard metallic object. A depression was visible in the soil, with a central hole three feet in diameter and three smaller indentations around it. They indicated the presence of a very heavy device. Furthermore, Cuban radar in the area had detected an unidentified object that vanished amidst a tremendous amount of electronic noise.

Within a fifteen-foot radius the soil at the site was calcined and covered with ashlike gray dust, which was duly analyzed without producing any unusual results: it only confirmed that a high degree of heat had been applied to the soil.

Soviet experts quickly deployed a veritable arsenal of measuring instruments and took many samples.

Thirteen days after the incident Puentes began

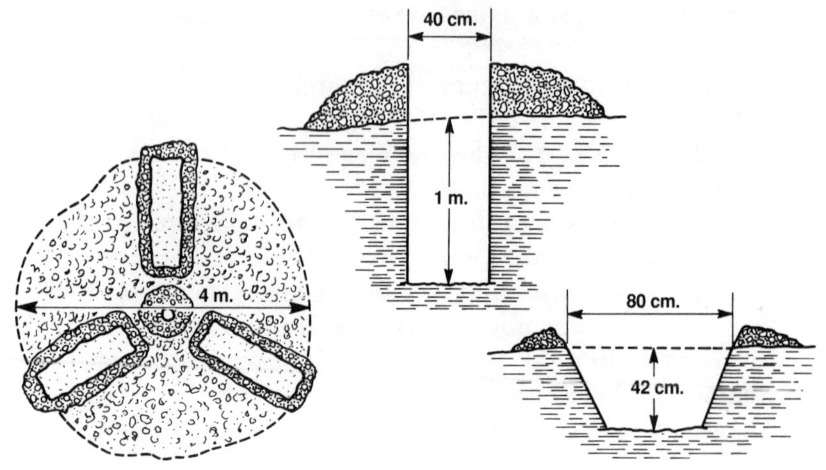

Fig. 6. Diagram of traces left by a UFO observed by Cuban army reservist Isidro Puentes Ventura. The incident was investigated by Soviet military experts.

awakening from the coma. He told doctors and military officials that he had first seen a white light behind some trees. He went to investigate and found himself 150 feet away from an object that was resting on the ground. He observed it for ten minutes. It was round, with a dome and a series of "antennas" on top. In spite of the strange shape and unusual brilliance of the object, Puentes came to the conclusion that the craft must be an American helicopter (what else could it be?) and started firing at it, as he had been instructed and trained to do. He had fired about forty rounds when the craft became orange and emitted a strong whistling sound. That sound was his last conscious memory.

When they heard this story, Soviet intelligence

experts escalated the study of the case. Puentes was subjected to intense interrogation for fifty hours, then sent to a group of psychiatrists for further testing. These examinations simply confirmed that Isidro Puentes was a normal, reliable, uneducated Cuban peasant. There was no contradiction in his story, no matter how often he was questioned about it.

Next, the witness was put through fifteen hypnosis sessions, during which he told the same exact story everybody had already heard. And the fourteen flattened bullets whose trajectory had been dramatically interrupted by some very hard and smooth object were further evidence of his veracity.

In spite of such cases, the director of Pulkovo Observatory, Vladimir Alexeyevich Krat, stated in July 1978 that the UFO problem boiled down to two parts: first, natural phenomena that were poorly studied; second, classical objects in space such as artificial satellites. Krat bitterly criticized Azhazha and Professor Veynik of the Bielorussian Academy of Sciences for lecturing on the subject, and he went on to declare that "there is no real evidence to show that there is life, including intelligent life, anywhere but on planet earth."[27]

In January 1979, the pressure from the sheer number of UFO sightings became such that scientific authorities felt obligated to act. Two distinguished scientists, Vladimir Migulin and Platov, published an important article in the magazine *Nedelya* in response to a man from Kuybychev (on the Volga, some 500 miles east-southeast of Moscow) who had reported a UFO.[28] Noting that the Academy of Sciences was receiving numerous such reports, they enumerated all the natural phenomena that could explain them.

However, they also conceded that some reported sightings did remain unidentified and were worthy of calm and sober scientific research. They concluded their paper with some technical advice to the readers of the review on proper ways to report future sightings, asking that they be forwarded to the Academy of Sciences.

During our visit to Moscow we were able to meet with Professor Migulin (see Chapter 14). He told us frankly that he remained very skeptical about the reality of the reported sightings.

In spite of the new willingness of scientific authorities to consider the sightings and to analyze them, the road to full scientific acceptance of the phenomenon is going to be a long and arduous one. And the burden is on us to convince our colleagues, to educate them about the seriousness of the UFO experience, and to go on with our own research into the unknown.

CHAPTER 8

BIOLOCATION: CAN UFO ANOMALIES BE DETECTED BY HUMANS?

Every living entity generates a biological field. It is probably an attribute of the organic realm. Perhaps it is when it learned to generate this field that nature became alive.

Professor Alexis Zolotov
Moscow, January 1990

Many incidents of our trip to the Soviet Union were so powerful that they have remained fixed in my memory. Among them was the experience of watching Professor Alexis Zolotov walking up and down the length of the carpeted office of the vice-chairman of Novosti holding a strange metallic contraption ahead of him. His bright eyes and long, wiry gray beard completed the illusion of some age-old, esoteric ceremony as the metal wire in his hand twisted repeatedly to the left and to the right, as if moved by a definite but invisible force of nature.

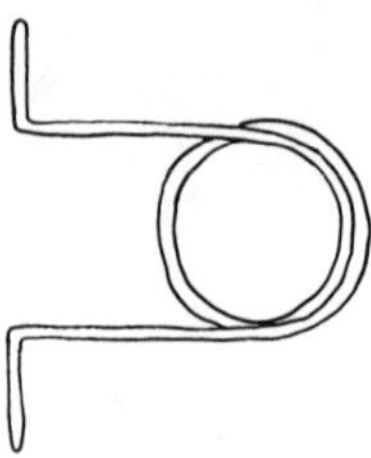

Fig. 7. Shape of the dowsing device used by Alexis Zolotov in biolocation tests.

"The desk should not be here," announced the scientist. "This is a negative section of the room. You can verify this yourselves."

Martine got up and took hold of the device as instructed. She walked along the wall and felt the wire twist in her hand. I did the same with obvious results. But this was hardly a scientific experiment. Perhaps we had been unconsciously influenced by watching Zolotov's earlier performance. In any case, the time had clearly come to learn more about a phenomenon all Soviet ufologists seemed to take for granted, the effect of biolocation, which had created such confusion in the West when Tass had first revealed its use in Voronezh.

BIOLOGICAL FIELDS

"It is impossible to deny the existence of certain fields around living beings," said Alexis Zolotov as we sipped our morning tea, which had already become a cherished tradition.

"The word *field* is pretty vague in this context," I pointed out. "It's all a question of definition."

"Of course," answered Zolotov. "And some people

use terms like *aura*, which are even more vague. We currently have two schools of thought in Russia on this point. Some people argue that we are dealing with the fusion of known phenomena like the electric field, the magnetic field, and so on, which change in quality when they are mixed together. The second group believes that the aura actually corresponds to an independent physical field, not yet recognized, but endowed with its own characteristics. I must tell you that I lean toward the latter view."

While the people around the table lit their cigarettes and prepared to take notes, Zolotov made an additional comment. "Every living entity generates a biological field. It is probably an attribute of the organic realm. Perhaps it is when it learned to generate this field that nature became alive."

"So how would you characterize this new field?" I was eager to hear his answer.

Zolotov proved to be a patient teacher. "Let's talk about two of its major characteristics," he said. "I call them superimposition and induction. It is the superimposition or, more simply, the *fusion* of all these fields that constitutes the global field of the earth. But because of its unequal distribution over the planet the biological field presents certain anomalies."

"In the West one often hears claims about specific spots," I said. "Megalithic sites are supposed to be an example of such anomalies. Do you subscribe to this idea?"

"Yes. Such sites include natural features over which churches and temples were erected down through the centuries. We have a major anomalous zone in the Perm region."

"Is the anomaly generally of an energetic nature? Energy and information are two sides of the same coin. So why couldn't these effects be informational in nature? We may be missing a large part of the phenomenon."

Zolotov smiled. His answer indicated that he had thought long and hard about the same problem. "You will grant to me that for energy to be equated with information it must have a carrier, a vector. The problem is that we have not yet identified all the carriers. There are probably more than five levels, perhaps seven or nine. Level one is cinetic motion, which became understood in the eighteenth century. Level two is the electromagnetic field, which we mastered early in the present century. Now we are on the threshold of the third level, the biological field."

The obvious thought flashed through my mind. If there were extraterrestrial beings, or if nonhuman forms of consciousness were interacting with us, they probably would not use the primitive methods that projects like SETI (Search for Extraterrestrial Intelligence) have always assumed they would use. Why bother sending us radio signals that are physically crippled by unacceptable propagation limitations when we may be on the threshold of understanding much more significant, effective, immediate forms of information exchange?

Zolotov went on, now speaking with a passion that betrayed his long interest in the subject. "The fourth level, in my opinion, will turn out to be the informational field you are talking about. We don't know much about the fifth and higher levels. They may have to do with the cosmic realm."

"Why would such biological field anomalies play a role in the manifestations of the UFO phenomenon?" I asked.

"We do not know why, but that certainly seems to be the case in the Perm region. The problem is that we don't know if the anomalies are stable or not. We do think some positive anomalies are stable, at sites where ancient temples have been erected, for example. Even when the temple itself has since been destroyed. But the density of biological fields does change."

INDUCTION

"The primary field impacts the whole earth, but the organic realm is influenced by the biological field. These two quantities add their effects together."

"Would you expect crystals to manifest these effects in special ways?" Martine asked.

"Crystals are known to have particular properties with respect to electromagnetism, and they probably have similar advantages for the biological domain. One example comes to mind, that of a sensitive named Vanga who lives in Bulgaria. He is blind, but he seems to have a special ability to diagnose illnesses. He makes his patients simply hold a cube of sugar during the process because he says the sugar crystals confirm his readings. A minute ago you brought up the information field. It is possible that sensitive subjects simply read out this field. But do you realize that ten years ago we could not have had this conversation? People would have said we were dealing with mystical nonsense!"

"What happens if you actually create an artificial anomaly, for example, by damming a river, by altering the landscape?"

"If you introduce a new biological field," Zolotov

said, "new lines of force will be created, and they can be detected by people trained in biolocation. The sign will be positive in certain parts of the area and negative in others. Furthermore, there will be important transition zones in between."

"What do they mean? Assuming that you can reliably trace these lines of force, as you claim, how do you know what conclusions to draw from their existence?"

The answer seemed obvious to Zolotov. "The zones of negative force usually are experienced as discomfort, and the positive ones induce euphoria. Historically, religious authorities had placed their centers of worship on positive zones. But the transition regions are the most nefarious. To give you a simple example, in some houses we find that the bed is at the wrong place. This can cause illnesses, arguments between husband and wife. We try to remove negative fields from certain rooms or certain buildings. I have demonstrated to you what happened in this office where we are now," he added, motioning toward the desk and drawing invisible lines of separation through the room. "But some of the most important applications are to enclosed spaces where people have to work together, such as submarines and space stations."

"The use of the word *field* implies more than simple detection," I argued. "It suggests the ability to focus, to concentrate, to broadcast, and to modify. Have you explored these possibilities in the laboratory?"

"Yes, and we know the field can be concentrated. We can take a watch, for example, and act on its internal mechanism."

"Even a digital watch?"

"Yes. One can affect the quartz crystal inside the watch, of course."

"I suppose this applies to the human body as well?" asked Martine.

"There have always been healers who treated diseases by such means, in Russia and elsewhere, but that is not a simple situation. The healers often make predictions; they claim to see the future. If that is true, they must be accessing the informational field as well."

This last remark launched us into a discussion of the nature of time. In modern physics it is generally argued that time is a dimension similar to the three dimensions of space, and common logic is based on the assumption that effects always derive from causes. I confessed to Zolotov that I had drifted away from theoretical physics when I began doubting that it could account for psychic reality. If time is a dimension like any other, why can we only move in one direction along the time axis? Such topics were never discussed. The very concept is too narrow, especially if one takes into account paranormal experiments where sensitive subjects have reliably acquired information about the future.

"Such experiments have been done so successfully that they can no longer be ignored," I emphasized.

Zolotov responded with the indulgence of a cardinal confronted by a young priest who had just posed a nagging question to him about the nature of the angels. Again, it was clear that he represented a group of scientists who had pondered these problems and had recognized the obvious fact that modern physics will face major changes if information can be retrieved from the future, or if it has failed to take into account biological fields that are everywhere around us. Zolotov also gave me to understand that this was neither the time nor the place to go deeper into such a vast problem.

"Have you read the works of Hegel?" he asked. "He tried to explain the paranormal phenomena of his time, such as mesmerism and clairvoyance. But he could not account for precognition. We continue this research . . . we have many subjects who can do these things."

PRACTICAL APPLICATIONS

We continued to seek answers. "If I understand you correctly, you have not only studied these various fields, but you are actually using this knowledge in practical applications. Can you describe them?"

"Everything we do has practical applications," Zolotov said. "Our institute in Kalinin is concerned with mineral exploration. Our students are geologists, and they graduate with a diploma in biolocation."

"You mean . . . an official diploma?" asked Martine with a note of astonishment in her voice.

"Yes, yes. Everything in the USSR is official, you know," remarked Zolotov, his eyes sparkling with humor. "We are part of the Department of Geology, what you would call the Department of the Interior, and we have a state budget."

"If you take a group of average geologists, how many of them have the ability to learn biolocation?" Martine inquired.

"Most people have, in varying degrees. The vast majority can be trained. Our students are not parapsychologists, mind you. They use what we teach them to go into the field and find mineral deposits. You should come and visit us. Kalinin is only two hours away by train."

"So how do you apply these techniques to the study of UFOs?" I asked.

"And how did you personally become involved in this?" added Martine.

"When I was researching the Tunguska catastrophe I witnessed UFOs three times," answered Zolotov. "They looked like orange-colored globes. They were silent, with an arc of light around them. In 1976 I saw a luminous cylinder in the sky."

"Can you give us examples of close encounters from your files?"

"Let me tell you about two specific landing cases where I have visited the actual sites. The first one was at Octobriski, in the Bakhiri Republic. That was in April 1967. We found a large hole in the ground. It measured nineteen feet in diameter, and it was perfectly round. We computed that twenty tons of dirt had been removed by an unknown phenomenon."

"Were there any witnesses?"

"Yes, they told us they had seen a large cloud, and when it dissipated they found this hole. We eliminated both the lightning bolt theory and the meteorite hypothesis."

Zolotov paused to give us time to take notes, then he went on. "Ten years later, in August 1977, in Chekhov, near Serpukhov, three friends were gathering mushrooms when all of a sudden they noticed something like a bright sphere or balloon. But it wasn't just a balloon, because at the site was a depression fourteen feet in diameter. It was not deep, only two inches, but the depression was equivalent to a resting mass of 2,000 tons. The dirt was sterile at the spot, with a significant drop in the number of microorganisms."

Taking a map where we had circled the town of Chekhov, Zolotov tapped it with his finger for emphasis. "This is the first case where biolocation was used by our investigators. Our greatest specialists went there. When I visited the site, it must have been a year later, the dowsing instrument was still spinning very hard."

I had to clarify the implications of such a phenomenon. "Does that indicate anything in particular to you?"

"The strength of the fixed field," answered Zolotov.

"Is that true for every subject?" I asked in some surprise.

"Of course. When several specialists investigate the sites, they generally observe the same manifestations."

That was one of the points that gave me the most trouble. While there is a long tradition of dowsing in the West, supported by preliminary but tantalizing laboratory research, various investigators generally experience the phenomenon in different ways, not in the neat and reliable fashion the Soviet researchers seemed to be describing.

"So please explain to me how that relates to the presence of a UFO," I said to Zolotov.

"Well, in both cases we had to conclude that the phenomenon had affected the biological field very deeply. The signals we record at such places are unlike those that occur naturally. They fall into a characteristic pattern we have learned to recognize."

PERSONAL OBSERVATIONS

It was left for Martine to pose the question that would reveal for us how closely the UFO phenomenon in the Soviet Union had followed the same patterns observed in the West. "Other than those globes of light in Siberia," she asked, "have you had any direct experience?"

Alexis Zolotov just smiled and answered her, a touch of self-consciousness sneaking for the first time into his voice. "I saw a humanoid when I was seven, in 1933. This happened in the house where I was born. He appeared very suddenly in the room where I was standing. This being had a high cranium, no mask or breathing apparatus. He was as tall as a man. He looked at me and I looked at him for maybe ten seconds, from fifteen feet away. His head was three times larger than a human's. He had large pointed ears. His face was covered with fine wrinkles, and his eyes conveyed great intelligence and a lack of emotion. He had the look of a very old man. I ran away . . ."

"Out of fear?"

"Not really—I can't explain it. I didn't know what else to do."

"Did you tell the story to anyone?" asked Martine.

"I told my parents about it. They laughed at me. So I never mentioned it again for forty-two years."

CHAPTER 9

AN EVENING WITH ALEXANDER KAZANTSEV

There is not a single fact that would indicate that secret material objects which have been called *disks* or *saucers* are flying above us. All conversations in this regard, which have recently received such wide dissemination have the same source: the unconscionable and anti-scientific statements made in Moscow by irresponsible persons. These reports relate fantastic fairy tales taken primarily from the American Press. The American astronomer [Donald] Menzel devoted an entire book to an examination of this question and came to the conclusion that flying saucers are nothing but an optical effect.

Academician Y. A. Artsimovich
Pravda, *January 8, 1961*

The serious investigator must be mindful of the fact that there is no place for either blind credence or blind denial in science. It is extremely difficult to interpret objective sightings as ordinary natural phenomena. It seems to the authors of the present article that the time has come to give serious consideration to the space hypothesis about UFOs. They may be piloted by intelligent beings or by *thinking* cybernetic machines.

Alexander Kazantsev and Jacques Vallee
Trud *(Labor), August 24, 1967*

My correspondence with the writer Alexander Kazantsev goes back to 1966. Together we had broken the barrier of skepticism to coauthor an article that caused a sensation in the Soviet Union when it appeared in *Young Technology Magazine* the following year.[29] It was the first article in Russian arguing for the physical reality of unidentified flying objects.

A magazine devoted to scientific speculation for students, *Young Technology Magazine* has a circulation comparable to *Popular Mechanics*. But our article was quickly picked up and reprinted by *Trud*, the daily newspaper of the Soviet labor unions, with a circulation of 22 million. When news of it spread, that issue of *Trud* was snatched off the streets by a public starved for information about UFOs. It became a collectors' item and remains the most widely circulated piece ever published on the subject of UFOs.

I had never met face-to-face with Alexander Kazantsev. Thus it was with considerable trepidation that I climbed the stairs to his apartment near Moscow University in January 1990. I reviewed in my mind his literary achievements. Born in 1906, in Akmolinsk in Siberia, two years before the famous Tunguska catastrophe, he had graduated from the Tomsk Technological Institute in 1930. He was the author of such best-sellers as *The Blazing Island*, *Northern Jetty*, and *Arctic Bridge*. He was a widely read popularizer of space science and a revered science fiction author.

It was also Kazantsev who, in 1946, put forward the hypothesis that the Tungus object was a spaceship fueled by antimatter. Publication of this theory had started an intense debate among Russian intellectuals. The skeptics had never forgiven him, but to many young researchers he had been a light in the fog, an inspiration.

Martine and I had a pleasant surprise when Kazantsev opened his door and ushered us into his study: Alexis Zolotov was there, smiling and relaxed. The two were old friends, we learned. Zolotov's imagination had been ignited as a young geologist when he read Kazantsev's hypothesis about Tunguska.

"Seeing that article was the turning point in my life," Zolotov said as we sat comfortably, our backs to the book-laden shelves that extended from wall to wall and from floor to ceiling.

It felt warm and cozy in Alexander Kazantsev's study. It was the world of a writer. For decades it had been a focus for letters, reports, books, and photographs from all over the globe.

"That paper we published together back in the sixties caused quite a stir, didn't it?" I said. Kazantsev laughed, stroking his white goatee. That gesture seemed to remind him of something.

"You've worked closely with Allen Hynek. I never had a chance to meet the man, but they say that I look like him. Tell me, is that true?"

I had to admit there was a strong resemblance, not only because of the old-fashioned goatee, but also the professional air, and the glint of irony or humor in the eye. Kazantsev was obviously pleased at the fact that he might be a mirror image of the American astronomer. He poured us some cognac and we started gossiping like old friends, without any agenda, any fixed plan or purpose.

SPECULATIONS ABOUT TWO SIBERIAN CRASHES

"So, how long have you two worked together?" I asked.

"Alexis and I started collaborating in 1959 in our study of the Tunguska phenomenon," answered Kazantsev.

"As you know, there were several expeditions," broke in Zolotov. "One of them was organized by a man named Korolev. Researchers were fully prepared to discover the remains of a Martian spacecraft! But there was nothing at the site, nothing at all."

"Until they found that strange piece of metal in 1975, near the Varta River, in the north country," pointed out Kazantsev.

"What kind of metal did they recover?" I asked. "Was it analyzed?"

"Oh, yes, but that took a while. It was silvery and it looked like something that had been manufactured—like a tube or a collar. Ten years later it was brought back to Moscow and an Academy of Sciences lab finally analyzed it. They found it was an alloy of some rare elements: 67 percent cesium with 10 percent lanthanum and some neodymium. How these components had been fused together was a mystery."

Kazantsev launched into a very technical description that our interpreter had difficulty in following, so I will not hazard to transcribe it here in detail. He did, however, say that later studies had shown the object to have a magnetic anomaly: the magnetic field was stronger on one side than on the other, by a factor of fourteen. And the site where it was found was in line with the trajectory of the Tunguska phenomenon.

"One possible hypothesis is that we are dealing with a piece of the object, whatever it was."

"Yours is such a disconcerting country," remarked Martine, "with such a surprising approach to technology."

"We have followed our own path in technology," Kazantsev said. "Don't forget that as early as 1910 a Russian engineer named Tsander proposed an electroplane based on the law of interaction between electricity and magnetism. The following year Karalin was on the threshold of using superconductivity. . . . You might ask, thinking back to the tales of Jonathan Swift: how can the island of Laputa fly? Well, the island of Laputa can fly if it has a huge superconductive coil to store electrical energy and it interacts with the earth's magnetic field, naturally . . ."

"But aircraft technology went in a different direction," pointed out Zolotov.

"Who was Tsander?" I asked.

"He worked with Konstantin Tsiolkowski. Well, his work takes us back to the Tunguska object. What if UFOs are some sort of electrical craft? Perhaps the larger vessels stay in orbit. What we see is only the landing module. Perhaps the object that exploded in 1908 was the big mother ship. In 1967 an astronomer named John Bigby claimed to have cataloged ten small satellites of the earth that were neither Russian nor American . . . that was published in *Icarus*. He suggested they might have originated from a single body that exploded about December 18, 1955. But that would have been two years before Sputnik!"

"Perhaps it was in orbit since 1908!" I exclaimed. "Is that what you're suggesting?"

"Yes. Perhaps they had planned the explosion."

"But during those forty-seven years astronomers should have seen the craft in question up in the sky. I mean, if it was that big . . ."

"Not necessarily. Perhaps it was painted black. That would make sense, if it stored thermal energy. Remember the early stories about a Black Knight in space?"

Martine and I did recall some speculation about a dark satellite, in the early years of the space program. Rumors about such an object had been sensationalized by the media, but nothing concrete had been found. This brought to mind a more recent event.

"The Western press has mentioned another object that seems to have crashed near Dalnegorsk, on January 29, 1986. Have you looked into that report?" I inquired.

"Yes, yes. We have a direct contact with the people who have studied the thing, of course." Kazantsev shrugged. "But it has a complex, artificial structure. Under the microscope you can see a mesh with fine gold thread."

"Then it could be the remains of a sophisticated electronic system that was destroyed by heat or an explosion, don't you think?"

"Yes, it may have been made on earth. There is no indication of nonhuman origin, although its exact nature remains a mystery."

Our interpreter told us that a piece of the Dalnegorsk object was preserved at the Cosmos UFO exhibit in Moscow, and that arrangements would be made for us to see and touch it.

ANCIENT STATUES AND MODERN BUREAUCRACIES

The rest of the evening was spent reminiscing about the politics of UFO research and the Stoliarov period. Kazantsev had worked closely with Felix Zigel until his death. "The Stoliarov committee lasted only a month or so, in 1967, then it was suddenly closed," he told us. "What an opportunity wasted for good research!"

We speculated about the real reasons for the desire by the authorities, both in the Soviet Union as in the United States, to discourage open research about the UFO phenomenon. Bureaucracies are closed to such inquiries under any political regime. That, we agreed, was one of the major lessons one could draw from the UFO enigma. There is little room for completely free inquiry in modern science.

More cognac was served and Alexander Kazantsev opened the glass doors of a bookcase to take down a series of remarkable statuettes from ancient Japan. They showed strange beings with goggles and a breathing apparatus.

"Were they primitive human warriors?" Kazantsev asked. "Or were they space explorers? This phenomenon seems to have been with us throughout history," added our host.

We agreed that prospects for the future of this research were as clearly delineated as the mystery it presented for our science. When we finally understand the nature of UFOs, many of our ideas about ourselves and our place in the world will have to change.

Perhaps it is this fundamental change in man's awareness of his true place in nature that authorities are trying to postpone at all cost until they can fully control it. There is no model in society's experience for the peaceful contact between mankind and another form of conscious intelligence. Ufologists in all countries, with all the inadequacies of their training, with all the limitations of their methods, may be the first group of people to ask these fundamental questions.

Perhaps, for a long time to come, the debate will have to be pursued in such settings: in quiet, warm conversations around a table strewn with books, maps, and ancient artifacts; in private homes where individual researchers using their own resources have accumulated a lifetime of intriguing records that all the major centers of learning have ignored.

After we left Kazantsev's apartment, as we bundled up against the fierce cold and began a futile search for a taxi along the deserted avenue, it was hard not to reflect again how fragile such research was, how strongly it rested on friendship and trust, and on a common passion for truth among a very small group of individuals spread over several continents.

CHAPTER 10

CITY OF THE STARS

> Two hundred years ago, when science rejected the reality of meteorites, the innate sluggishness of our thinking and the deficiency of our knowledge hampered the truth. But if we agree that the past may be instructive for the present, we cannot reject certain facts simply because they do not conform to currently accepted impressions of the world. Nature is preparing many more surprises for mankind and we must always be ready for them.
>
> *Professor Felix Zigel*
> *Moscow, February 1968*

There was a strange character who haunted the hallways of our hotel. One night he approached us, practically demanding that we change some dollars against his rubles.

A cluster of such individuals—pimps and petty crooks, informers, undercover cops—loitered at every entrance to the huge hotel, and we had to elbow our way through their group to get out, showing our guest cards to the guards. Evidently there is a black market in guest cards, explained the Novosti men, as they took us to a chauffeured car for a trip beyond the borders of Moscow.

Only a few years ago the training center for Soviet cosmonauts—the prestigious City of the Stars—was strictly off-limits to foreigners and to ordinary Soviet citizens themselves. It was a secret, self-contained complex where test pilots, scientists, and cosmonauts lived with their families. In recent years a more liberal approach was established. It was no longer compulsory for families to live cloistered behind the fence, in the multistoried buildings where Yuri Gagarin and all the early pioneers of Soviet space science had once made their homes.

All this was explained to us by our guides as we drove for nearly an hour through the Moscow traffic jams, passing long, slow lines of uniformly green, sturdy Soviet trucks. New snow was falling, putting a happy frame of white on the green and blue painted wood of the ornamented dachas that belonged to the more fortunate suburbanites. Some of the buildings exhibited fancy gingerbread that would have been at home in the Victorian-era sections of San Francisco.

Eventually we found ourselves driving on a modern, straight road with woods on both sides. We reached a crossroads where a MiG jet fighter was pointing at the sky, projecting from a huge concrete pedestal. We turned away from the highway and entered a large complex. Our identities were carefully checked at the guardhouse. A few minutes later we had penetrated a different world, the inner sanctum of Soviet high tech. The chauffeur parked the car in fresh, ankle-deep snow in front of the main building where dozens of cosmonauts had received their basic training.

THE COSMONAUT TRAINING CENTER

As we stepped into the building with our guides (an officer of the center had now joined our Novosti interpreter), we were all aware that we were not entering just another scientific institute. The Soviet Union has placed a high priority on space research, and it has not wavered in its determination since the fifties. While the United States and Europe went through periods of high investment (and high achievement) in space research followed by long stretches of utter apathy, the managers of the Soviet plan went ahead with unrelenting energy. As a result, although they lagged in many high-technology fields and never repeated the American feat of landing on the moon, they had accumulated twice the experience of the United States in terms of weeks, months, and years of spaceflight.

The man who greeted us at the center was Valentin Zudov, a veteran cosmonaut who was now in charge of the training program, sometimes serving as a member of a backup team.

"I flew aboard Soyuz," he explained in response to one of Martine's questions. "Our flight had complex technical problems and we had to abort after two days in space. We landed in a lake."

Zudov made it clear that the experience had left him awed with the difficulties and the dangers of space flight. How appropriate, we reflected, to place at the head of the training program a man who had had firsthand experience with the limitations of the pilots and of the hardware, a man who had stared at the possibility of death in orbit.

With Zudov as a guide, we visited laboratories and testing rooms. We saw the various models of space suits used in extravehicular activities, and we stopped on a wide gallery that overlooked a full-scale duplicate of the Mir space station.

"Two of our cosmonauts have now been aboard Mir for 164 days," Zudov said proudly. "What you see down there is not a mock-up, it is the twin brother of the actual station. We use it for every test, every maneuver, every program, before we send instructions to duplicate the same motion in space."

PSYCHIC FUNCTIONING

As a journalist who specialized in covering space developments, Martine had many questions about the Soviet program. She found an atmosphere of frankness and candor that she had rarely experienced before.

This, in turn, encouraged me to ask about an aspect of the cosmonauts' activities that had never been mentioned publicly, to my knowledge. "Do you use parapsychological techniques as part of the training?" I bluntly asked Zudov.

A year or so before, I have no doubt the question would not have been answered. The interpreter might even have thought it unnecessary to translate it. Instead, Zudov smiled and told me without any reticence: "We only bring in parapsychologists to help in training for the long-duration flights, when we need to achieve the best meditation and concentration abilities."

It was my turn to smile as I imagined what might happen if I posed the same question to NASA officials in the United States, or to CNES in Paris. (During the Apollo program, astronaut Edgar Mitchell did conduct some personal experiments in telepathy from orbit, but NASA always declined to admit there might be something to psychic functioning.)

"Is hypnosis used in combination with psychic training?" I asked Zudov.

"No, we do not do anything that might impede the free functioning of the brain."

We also discussed the specific problems of long-duration flights, a subject that has been minimized in the press. We were told frankly that even after a year crew members had not completely returned to normal. It is standard practice for cosmonauts to have children before such missions rather than after, for fear of genetic malformations in later births. Several Soviet cosmonauts, notably Titov, have spent over a year in space.

We found the same attitude of pragmatic frankness when it came to the UFO subject. "There are many reports of unexplained phenomena in the atmosphere," said Zudov. "Unfortunately, none of our cosmonauts ever observed them from orbit, although some have seen UFOs from the ground."

When we asked for details we were told that cosmonaut Nicholas Provotkin had seen a series of bright spheres in 1978. They seemed equipped with winglike appendages. Similarly, it seems that none of the U.S. astronauts has actually observed a UFO from orbit, although Gordon Cooper told me that he had watched some flying craft he could not recognize when he was a test pilot. He was on the ground at the time.

This led us to a discussion about the possibility of discovering intelligence in the cosmos. Our Soviet hosts said they were increasingly optimistic, citing observations of planetlike masses near Vega recently made by a Norwegian satellite. The search for life in deep space is clearly one of the intellectual motivations behind the Soviet program.

THE SPACE STATION

We went downstairs to the floor of the huge hangar to walk around the space station, which was made up of components that can be assembled at various docking rings and connected through hatches and airlocks. The only people we saw aboard the station were computer programmers. They were developing new software for the experiments conducted in orbit. The programs would be beamed up (one could hardly speak of downloading) to the space station.

The visit was continued with a tour of the training facility for extravehicular activities—in other words, complex excursions in space. The facility consisted of a large water tank, twenty-three meters in diameter, housed in a special building. When fully suited, the cosmonauts are in perfect equilibrium within the tank, which contains 5,000 cubic meters of water. We watched typical training sessions on videotape, after which we looked through the portholes of the huge tank itself.

Spacecraft mock-ups allow the cosmonauts to practice opening and closing hatches, going out of the Mir space station, and performing such delicate tasks as deploying solar panels.

"Each cosmonaut goes through twelve or thirteen such sessions," we were told. "And it is typical for them to lose six pounds in four hours, the duration of each session."

Oddly enough, in the midst of these high-tech wonders, we were most impressed by the simple display of two old space capsules from the earliest manned flights. They had been brought back from their landing sites, all burned and black from their fiery reentry, and sat on the floor of the Mir facility. Next to the space station, whose majestic structures towered above them, they looked ludicrously small and fragile. The image that came to mind as we touched the charred metal of the cone-shaped capsules that peeled off under the hand was that of Jules Verne's lunar explorers, which he had imagined shot out of the mouth of a giant cannon—a testament to an era of metallurgy and the brute force of progress, of incredible adventure and individual courage. With their tiny windows and the huge thickness of their skin they seemed to have been winched up from the depth of the sea rather than picked up from the snow like the artificial meteorites they actually were.

Martine and I had seen actual spacecraft on several occasions, but always before they had been launched. We were not fully prepared for the sight of the crazy machines when they came back to earth.

Here, again, the lesson was clear. A man had actually inhabited this tiny cone of burning metal as it descended through the atmosphere, surrounded by glowing plasma, unable to communicate by radio with the crews that were supposedly waiting to recover him alive. And that was the lesson men like Zudov wanted their students to learn. Astronautics 101 began with a tour of burned-out hardware that had nothing pretty about it. All the glamour, all the superficial glory, all the mythology had been stripped and blasted off the skin of those capsules on the way down. What was left was a basic combination of raw metal and pure human courage.

We ended our visit to the City of the Stars with a few quiet moments in the former office of Yuri Gagarin, the first man in space.

Upon his return to earth, Gagarin had been made a hero of his country, honored by Nikita Khrushchev and given a special office that was preserved exactly as it was on the day of his death. It is a simple but large rectangular room, with a map of the world on the back wall and a plain wooden desk. Perpendicular to the desk is a small meeting table with four chairs. It has become a tradition for cosmonauts to spend some time in personal meditation, sitting at that table before leaving on a mission, aware that they might be living their last hours on planet earth.

I found the experience strangely moving. And in response to Martine's questions, we learned some of the details of Gagarin's death. The world had been told that he had crashed during a routine training flight, at the controls of a MiG. What the world had not been told was that he was drunk at the time. He plowed through the trees and crashed in the nearby forest.

"He lost sight of what it meant to be a mere mortal," our guide told us sadly. "He was hailed everywhere as a hero, the first man in space. He thought he could do anything, dare anything, always go farther . . ."

There is a dramatic photograph on the wall of Gagarin's office in the City of the Stars. It simply shows a plain clump of trees with their tops sheared off, under an empty sky. I am not ashamed to confess it: that poignant picture, more eloquent than a thousand speeches, brought tears to my eyes. It certainly explained why cosmonauts found it useful to spend some time in that office in meditation about the earth life they were leaving behind, and why the man in charge of their training was a veteran of a crippled spacecraft. During our visit to the City of the Stars we did not meet anyone who thought the path to the cosmos would be an easy one.

CHAPTER 11

UNDERGROUND: CONVERSATIONS AROUND A BOTTLE OF VODKA

> The Russian tradition of natural healing has always preserved the ancient ways under the Orthodox Church, under the tsar, and even under communism. . . . We're ahead of you in the study of the paranormal because the Western churches killed all your witches in the name of their dogma. You only have yourselves to blame if you have fewer gifted psychics. You've eliminated their genes from the gene pool.
>
> *Healers Eugene and Larissa Kolessov*
> *Moscow, January 1990*

"They have planned some boring meeting for you this evening," said one of the young journalist friends we had made at Novosti. "But it would be a lot more fun for you to meet some of our unconventional researchers."

We agreed to dump the official program and to go off into the cold night in search of the Soviet New Age. Soon we were seated around a large table in yet another cramped apartment, discussing the paranormal with two young practitioners, Eugene Kolessov and his wife, Larissa. In a corner of the room was a very modern-looking IBM personal computer clone, in the process of being repaired by a young technical wizard I will call Grishka.

A HOLISTIC PERSPECTIVE

"We started seven years ago," said Eugene. "We were trained in human science and philology, and it is an accident that decided our fate, when we found that we could heal pain by natural techniques, such as touching the patient's head. This led us in turn to study homeopathy and acupuncture."

Martine expressed surprise that such traditional forms of healing, which are often regarded in the West as little more than superstition, could have survived in the harsher political realities of the Soviet Union.

"Things are not as dark as they seem," answered Larissa. The Russian tradition of natural healing has always preserved the ancient ways under the Orthodox Church, under the tsar, and even under communism. "Homeopathy, historically, spread very widely through Germany and Russia. In the thirties one Soviet drugstore out of two sold homeopathic remedies."

"Don't forget that Stalin himself once ordered an experiment with 5,000 patients who had various illnesses," added Eugene. "Half were treated with homeopathy, the others with classical techniques. The results were inconclusive when an assessment was made after one year. Many of the patients treated by homeopathy were found to be cured, but the medical profession claimed they must have recovered spontaneously. The influence of homeopathy diminished but was never eliminated; today you can still find one clinic and six pharmacies in Moscow that are dedicated to it. We feel these techniques apply best to children and to older people."

Around the room were many shelves with books. It was obvious that knowledge was revered here to a degree that our information-saturated world had forgotten. The West is spoiled with the richness of its media, and it is losing the ability to preserve some important insights. Unless an idea is presented in a package that can be neatly marketed and can fit nicely on the bookstore's shelf, it does not actually reach the average person. Russia has never had such a distribution system. Instead, ideas percolated among students, scholars, and private groups who created a veritable cult around the books that influenced them. This is the way it may have been in Western Europe before the invention of mass media, I found myself musing. In the eighteenth and nineteenth centuries, when there were still such things as genuine intellectual movements, and when new ideas were debated rather than mass marketed and hammered into the public's mind by television, this is what every evening with intelligent friends must have been like.

Some of the shelves did not hold books but boxes of medication, most of them based on herbal remedies that were as old as the oldest medical treatises. There were rules for taking such remedies, we were told, and they had to do with certain astrological conditions.

When I told our hosts that from my own observations I thought astrology was a flawed system, Larissa shook her head and gently argued. "Astrology is a science of man, not a science of the sky. All the sciences of man are interrelated."

"Astrology is akin to sociopsychology," Eugene added. "It is not an exact science. It has to do with the behavior of large masses of people. Matter, energy, and information are related," he went on, going back to the argument we had begun with Zolotov, and with the group from Voronezh.

"Is that what is creating so much interest in what you call biolocation?" I wanted to know.

"We experience it every day. For example, Grishka, here, knows how to create a psychic imprint in a stone by fixing his sight on it—or into it. But it turns out that water is the best medium to fix information."

"We never expected to find such a high level of interest in the paranormal in the Soviet Union," I told our hosts as I looked at the hundreds of books along the shelves. The topics they covered ranged from astrology and healing to spiritism and psychic research.

"Is that due to something about Russian traditions?" asked Martine. "Clearly, it is rooted at a level that political systems could not touch."

"We're ahead of you in the study of the paranormal because the Western churches killed all your witches in the name of their dogma," answered Eugene. "You only have yourselves to blame if you have fewer gifted psychics. You've eliminated their genes from the gene pool."

"How does that explain that there would be so much acceptance of parapsychology as a field of research in your country, when it is still treated as a marginal or even flaky discipline in the West?" I inquired.

"When it was at the apex of its power the Western

church killed over three million witches in the name of God," continued Eugene. "In proportion to the overall human population at the time, this was a terrible, unforgivable genocide. Many of those who died at the hands of your priests were young women who had not produced offspring. We have done many bad things in Russia, but we have never hunted down witches on such a scale. Our gene pool is still rich in psychic ability."

This interpretation can be debated on historical grounds, however. My friend Larissa Vilenskaya, herself a gifted psychic researcher, has pointed out that in the Middle Ages witches were burned at the stake in Russia just as they were in Western Europe. In a letter to me she gave several examples.

> In 1227, four witches were put to the flames in the court of an archbishop in Novgorod. In the beginning of the fifteenth century ten sorcerers were destroyed in Pskov. In a tale about witches written for Ivan the Terrible, fire was prescribed as the proper punishment for witchcraft.

Vilenskaya even quoted a disgruntled seventeenth-century Russian who spied for Sweden. In a report for his new employer he described witchcraft practices in Russia, adding that women were sometimes buried up to their breasts and left to die for their occult practices.

Vilenskaya's speculation on the large number of psychics in the Soviet Union is more pragmatic. "Because parapsychological research has been kept underground so long, there has been virtually complete silence in the press, with little pro or con debate." As a result, the Soviet public has not been exposed to as much exaggeration, false claims, and negative publicity as the Western audience. "People allowed themselves to function psychically," she concluded, "or more precisely, did not prevent themselves from manifesting these abilities because of negative cultural conditioning."

During my stay in Moscow I thought it was an ironic contradiction to see the materialistic society of the Soviet Union running out of food and material goods, while in the idealistic West supermarket shelves were bending under the weight of every delicacy and every possible gadget. Yet it was in the Soviet Union that spirituality seemed to thrive, among people who had an almost instinctive grasp of issues Western scientists were trying so hard to define.

TOWARD THE TWENTY-FIRST CENTURY

The time was getting late and the world outside had long ago retired into silence and night. There is not much traffic along Moscow streets after the evening commute, and it was easy to forget the city. Larissa and Eugene produced an excellent dinner, which we ate by candlelight. We settled down for a long evening of conversation.

My notes become sketchy at this point, but I remember that the discussion ranged from the nature and meaning of UFOs to computers and high technology and back to the mysteries of biolocation. Much of it had to do with the future, a subject that fascinates mainstream Soviet intellectuals much more than it does contemporary Western thinkers. In the United States the futurist movement of the fifties and sixties, led by such people and organizations as Herman Kahn, author of *The Year 2000*, the Hudson Institute, the Rand Corporation, and the Stanford Research Institute (from which many other groups had spun off), had been gradually fragmented into an array of teams working out short-term technical forecasts that used the methodology these pioneers had created. Perhaps that was a measure of their success. But with better technical forecasting had come a loss of vision. Outside the New Age groups, whose outlook was made suspect by reliance on channeling and spirit guides, few people were left to ask why we should explore space, or what to do with population issues in the developing world. The day-to-day handling of such problems was left to major corporations, to industry groups, to the World Bank. Only in the growing concern for the environment was there an intense debate involving diverging visions of the future; but that debate, too, was becoming more and more political. The scientific issues were increasingly precise, but decisions were made in the voting booth, and they were swayed by a level of media bombardment that clouded all the issues.

The Soviets, on the other hand, still regarded the future with the somewhat naive passion of a Jules Verne or an H. G. Wells. To them, the existence of nonhuman consciousness was a key factor.

"It is the twenty-first century that will determine the key position of our race's ultimate destiny," said Larissa. "It will define mankind's place in the cosmos."

"And it may bring us into contact with alien races," added Eugene. "There must be other beings in the universe. They may have a form of consciousness higher than our own."

"Does that necessarily mean that the UFO phenomenon is caused by extraterrestrials?" I asked. "Do they necessarily have to be from another planet? Are they necessarily more evolved than we are?"

"No, of course not," said Larissa. "Perhaps the UFOs simply represent another form of our own existence here."

We asked her to clarify what she meant.

"Well, what we know about these beings is that they seem to be curious of us, yet their physical substance is different from ours . . . they could be related to the human soul, a reflection of a world beyond death."

Sensing our skepticism, Larissa added: "Look at poltergeist phenomena. Don't they seem to belong to the same class of unexplained effects caused by a consciousness that is close to the human realm?"

We never resolved that issue, although arguments were presented back and forth, invoking various hypotheses, and the reports of witnesses who had reported close encounters, abductions, and related anomalies.

Grishka, who had followed the debate from a corner of the room, broke into the conversation with an unexpected comment. "You know, there is a bias in these observations. Somebody has remarked that people often don't always report what they see. In fact, the more bizarre the sighting, the lower the chance they will make a report."

"Where did you find that observation?" I inquired, curious to learn who could have done this kind of research in the Soviet Union.

"Oh, I read it in a book I have. The author even gives a curve for this probability: people tend to report those sightings that are a little strange but not too strange. When they see something very close and very scary, they only tell their family."

"What's the title of that book?"

"It's called *The Invisible College.*"

That remark left us stunned. The interpreter explained to Grishka that I had written the book in question. In fact, I had a copy of *The Invisible College* with me that evening, which I intended as a gift for the Kolessovs.[30]

It was their turn to be speechless.

"How could you know about this book?" I asked Grishka. "None of my works have been translated into Russian."

"We know your works. They circulate here in samizdat form, underground. We type such books ourselves. We make copies. We pass them around."

Eugene enthusiastically produced a bottle of vodka, and we drank a toast to celebrate an evening that seemed blessed by interesting coincidences. Larissa went back to describing her personal interpretations of astrology and the specialized software they were designing to cast horoscopes. She computed the data she claimed was related to Martine's future and to mine. We spoke of the problems of the world, of Gorbachev, of the prospect for peace, of the great changes that were sweeping Europe. Someone quoted Dostoyevsky: "It is the tragic destiny of Russia to teach important lessons to the world, by showing it what it should not do!"

That poignant phrase remained with us as we left our new friends, aware that we had only begun our debate. But perhaps we will be able to resume it in the future.

When she calculated the planetary positions that she claimed could influence my life, Larissa predicted that I would return. "Destiny puts you at the right place," she said with a tone of complete certainty. I smiled and she added: "I am aware of your skepticism. But you will come back to Moscow."

AT THE EXHIBITION PARK

We were still thinking about Dostoyevsky's remark the next morning when we visited the permanent exhibition on Soviet achievements. It is situated in a large park, with various pavilions and buildings dedicated to the major fields of agriculture and industry, and linked together by a light rail system. I remembered visiting it with my wife at the time of the Moscow mathematics congress in 1966, and I was shocked at the changes. Some buildings were closed, many were dilapidated, and an atmosphere of utter desolation hung over the park, made even more dramatic by a new layer of crisp snow that crackled ominously under our boots.

Just as I was beginning to get depressed by the heaviness of the scene, however, an incident created a welcome diversion.

We had taken our seats in the open cars of the little train that went slowly through the park, and I found myself next to the ticket machine. Typical of the Soviet way of doing business, the machine was operated on a voluntary basis. It was little more than a coin box with a slot and a crank to dispense the tickets. Our guide had put a few kopeks into it and taken tickets for all of us.

At the next stop an old woman climbed aboard with

a small boy, probably her grandson. The first thing she did after she sat down was to thrust some kopeks into my hand; she was obviously expecting me to do something, speaking in Russian with impatient authority when I failed to react. After he stopped laughing, our Novosti interpreter explained to me that since I was seated next to the ticket machine it was now my responsibility to put kopeks into the slot and to crank out tickets.

Another stop, another group of grandmothers with laughing kids, another handful of kopeks, another incomprehensible series of commands in Russian. By now I knew what to do. I just fed the machine and gave out tickets.

"You see, I have only been in Moscow three days and already I have an important job," I told Martine proudly. "If the hotel never returns our passports, I can always stay here and perform a useful function."

The Russian kids heard us speaking in a funny language and laughed at us even harder, so that it was a very happy group of people that finally arrived at the Cosmos building.

When I had seen it in the sixties, the space exhibit housed replicas of *Sputniks* I and *II*, a few mock-ups of space capsules, and an incomplete model of a cosmonaut suit. With the greater policy of openness, many of the exhibits had changed. There were now actual space vehicles rather than fake ones, and the suits were real. (We had just seen and touched the latest models at the City of the Stars.) But there was another innovation, an entire section devoted to unidentified flying objects. The exhibit included photographs, paintings, books, and artifacts. It even covered such sociological phenomena as UFO cults and contactee mythology, which we were surprised to learn was also a factor in the USSR.

The topic of cults and other extreme belief systems linked to UFO contact is a touchy one with many students of the phenomenon. When I published *Messengers of Deception* in 1979, many ufologists (notably those who belonged to organized groups) reacted to the book with a level of anger that was out of proportion to the comments I had offered. After carefully studying several contactee organizations and occult groups, some of which I had actually joined for a short time, I had come to the conclusion that high-demand sects were a very significant component of UFO mythology, although they had no hard data and no insight into the actual nature of the phenomenon.

It is an observation that seems so obvious today that it no longer raises any arguments. At the time, however, *Messengers of Deception* made many ufologists squirm, perhaps because they had never realized that they themselves were driven by a deep-seated desire to believe in extraterrestrials.[31]

There is the truth we seek and the truth we need to believe in, and these two truths are not necessarily identical.

The same observation applied to the Soviet Union, where genuine UFO data are buried within hoaxes, undocumented tales, and an enormous mass of wishful thinking. There were people who were sincerely looking for the key to the UFO mystery, and there were some who had already found it, including a bearded character named Porphyry Ivanov who had started his own cosmic community. We were told that astronaut Edgar Mitchell had once visited with Ivanov and told him that he had "seen him on the Moon."

Whether this dialogue actually happened or was another example of the wild UFO rumors that circulate among the Soviet New Age, we were unable to verify. We did see photographs that showed Ivanov with his disciples running half-naked through the snow.

We were told there was another extraterrestrial cult of UFO worshippers based in Riga. Its leader is said to be retired teacher Zinaida Robertovna, but we were given no other details.

Several photographs in the exhibit showed truly unexplained phenomena. In conversations with the organizers, including Boris Churinov, we later learned that many of these reports were indeed based on fact.

A case that took place in Turgay, Kazakhstan, in late June 1979 provides a typical example. An unidentified object was seen by military personnel there, who reported it publicly. There was a children's holiday camp nearby, and several campers saw from five to eight dark beings chasing them. As in the Voronezh case, the beings were described as very tall. The children estimated their height at over ten feet, but a teacher who had also witnessed the incident gave a more modest figure, closer to eight feet. She was only forty-five feet away from the beings and described them as having three fingers and no thumb. Imprints on the ground were found, measuring about three feet in diameter.

Another case, on February 13, 1989, involved Soviet pilots flying near Yerenin. What they saw in the sky near them was a large dark blue dirigiblelike object with windows, reminiscent of the classic American case reported by airline pilots Chiles and Whitted.

Before we left the exhibition we were able to examine a fragment of the object that had crashed at

Dalnegorsk on January 29, 1986. That examination, although obviously cursory and informal, reinforced my impression that the object in question was an ordinary piece of human technology, although it certainly was intriguing. It contained lead and also some metallic-looking parts, which we were told resisted corrosion when exposed to acids. We could also see glass fibers with fine gold wiring, but none of that warranted a conclusion that we were dealing with an object manufactured by a higher intelligence, as our Soviet friends conceded.

There was quite a crowd at the UFO exhibit, and we met several people who came to us spontaneously with stories of their own as soon as they realized we were from the West. One man told us that in 1957, in New Earth (Novaya Zemtya), two men vanished under strange conditions and an object was seen taking off. The military looked for them without success. We were also told that the Institute for Space Research of the Soviet Ministry of Defense was quietly conducting its own active studies into UFO phenomena.

It is said that one chapter of a 1987 book by Pugatsch (*The Sky Without Mystery*) was censored because it mentioned a military case. In that incident a pilot managed to land after a midair collision with a UFO. One wing and a piece of a stabilizer had been damaged by a red spherical object fifteen feet in diameter, which actually circled the aircraft. The year of the encounter was 1978.

An even more dramatic case occurred at 4:10 A.M. on September 7, 1984, in Minsk. Two military pilots saw an object that hit them with a beam of light. One of the pilots died; the other managed to land the plane, although he had also suffered physiological effects from the light.

When we came out of the park our friends showed us a tall metallic structure. "Do you see this tower?" they asked. "It is a television antenna that broadcasts programs over the whole Moscow area. In August 1974 an unidentified object flew over it, and all television shows stopped for twelve minutes. Such things cannot be kept secret forever."

The case had never been published, never written about anywhere. Yet everybody knew about it.

As we drove back into the city, I remembered Larissa's comment from the previous night, when we had raised the last glass of vodka in her book-filled apartment: "Don't be surprised if so much knowledge continues to thrive underground here. After all, invisible colleges are second nature to us."

CHAPTER 12

THE SECRET CHRONICLES

On November 30, 1964, at 1500 hours universal time an unusual celestial object was observed at the Shemakhinsky Astrophysical Observatory of the Academy of Sciences of Azerbaijan. . . .

Astronomers M. Gadzhiyes and K. Gusev

On the evening of October 18, 1967, while it was still twilight, I went out on Pravda Street in Rostov-on-Don and I saw an object overhead. It was shaped like a disk or a sphere. *S. A. Alferov,*
dean of the Rostov Manufacturing Institute of Agricultural Machinery

Russia has been a secret country, closed to the rest of humanity, for as long as the world remembers. Politics is not the only factor here. Moscow was already an enigma when the tsars lived in the Kremlin. The sheer size of the continent, its dreadfully cold climate, its primitive communications network, and the complexity of the various dialects contributed to making the country a mystery even before the communist regime imposed rigid rules of secrecy on every aspect of its life.

The language itself poses a formidable barrier to the visitor. Nothing can be said simply in Russian. While anyone can learn to say hi, the most common form of greeting in America, there is no alternative word to the formal *Strazdvoistsie* exchanged by the Russians. Even more frustrating is the fact that no two people seem to pronounce it the same way. After a few days in Moscow I shortened it to *Ztrasditsi*, which most folks seemed to understand, but I never found out whether I had actually mastered another Russian word or whether my friends had simply adapted to my mistakes, politely forgoing earlier attempts to correct me.

THE SLIGHTEST WHISPER CAN BE HEARD

It is an intriguing paradox that parapsychology and the study of UFOs have flourished in the Soviet Union precisely because of censorship. Secrecy was so prevalent that alternative underground methods of communication had to be developed by those engaged in scientific research and by the intelligentsia in general. It was a matter of physical and intellectual survival to create unofficial networks, with the surprising result that truly significant data could be made known through the underground much faster than in the West, where everyone is constantly bombarded with irrelevant noise pumped into the free press system by affluent public relations agencies.

"I like working in Russia because the slightest whisper can be heard instantly," a reporter friend of mine who works for *Sixty Minutes* once told me. "In the

United States the greatest story in the world will be ignored unless it is backed up by a professional media team and a multimillion-dollar advertising budget."

This uncanny ability to screen and preserve valuable information is one of the few benefits Soviet citizens have derived from the social system imposed by the regime, and it is quickly vanishing under glasnost.

What happened to a Russian artist named Malichev is an interesting example of what we might call the Secret UFO Chronicles of the Soviet Union. His story had never been published anywhere until *Le Figaro* featured his encounters and his paintings in the article Martine wrote following our trip. But everyone we met in Moscow seemed to have heard of it.

THE CASE OF THE ARTIST, THE GHOST, AND THE THREE UFONAUTS

The date was July 21, 1975. Near the village of Solnechnogorsk, fifty miles from Moscow, Malichev was in the middle of a pasture quietly painting a landscape on a beautiful day. Suddenly, as Martine related:

> He had the feeling that someone was touching his shoulder. He turned around and, to his amazement, found himself facing an object resembling a flying saucer. In front of the craft were three beings: two men and a woman who spoke to him telepathically. The woman seemed to be the leader of the group. The object was a disk, nearly forty feet in diameter, with three antennas.

The artist understood the bizarre message to be: "You have a very stable psychological system, for an average man. Do you want to fly with us?"

"I am not ready for such a trip," said Malichev, who is a solid citizen with a great deal of Russian common sense.

Quoting from Martine's report on the case:

> The artist is a man of about forty, with blue eyes. He speaks calmly. As he shows me the drawings he made to describe his experience, he explains: "The woman climbed on board and the object flew off, changing shapes several times. When it landed again in the field, I don't know why, but I followed the beings inside the craft."

Malichev's observation is one of the cases that demonstrate polymorphism, in my opinion one of the principal arguments against the idea that UFOs are simply spacecraft from another planet. The disk divided itself into eight parts that reunited into a single block, turned into a torus, then a cylinder. By the time it landed it had once more assumed the usual shape of a garden-variety flying saucer.

Malichev remembers being taken to a planet with three moons. At one point while he was on board the craft a huge face looked at him through a screen. During the forty minutes' duration of the flight he also recalls seeing his best friend, who had recently died, among the beings he observed, "as if in a dream." He was too afraid to go close to him. The entire experience lasted two hours.

The beings showed the artist what they regarded as the three stages of life: a body, then the outline of the body only, and finally a single luminous point in the lower abdomen.

"Malichev has been subjected to psychiatric observation and to psychological analysis," explained Vladimir Azhazha, who has studied the case. "He was hypnotized twice. He was not drugged, alcoholic, or crazy. During those two hours something did happen to him, but what was it?"

The same question can be asked, of course, about many other UFO reports in the Soviet Union and elsewhere.

THE CASE OF THE FISHERMEN AND THE BURNING BEAMS

When a fiery sphere appeared over the village of Roboziero and flew over the district, it was seen by many people attracted by the loud sound it produced. It measured some 150 feet in diameter and emitted two fiery beams pointing forward over a distance of 150 feet. It passed over a lake where several fishermen suffered deep burns.

Was that another example of the overwrought Russian imagination seeking release from the stress of socialism? Or was it a case of a superheated tabloid Soviet press trying to emulate the *National Enquirer*? Hardly. For this report, with all its details, was entered into the records of the monastery of St. Cyril in 1663, forty years before the first newspaper appeared in Russia. The actual text is worth quoting in detail.

> To His Highness the Archimandrite Nikita, to His Eminence the Starets Paul, to their Highnesses the Starets of the Synod of St. Cyril Monastery, most Venerable lords, salutations from your humble servant Ivachko Rievskoi.
>
> The farmer Lievko Fiedorov, from the village of Mys, has related to me the following facts:

> On this Saturday the fifteenth day of August of the year 1663, the faithful from the district of Bieloziero had assembled in great number in the church of the village of Roboziero. While they were inside a great sound arose in the heavens and numerous people came out of God's house to watch it from the square. There, Lievko Fiedorov, the farmer in question, was among them and witnessed what follows, which for him was a sign from God.
>
> At noon a large ball of fire came down over Roboziero, arriving from the clearest part of the cloudless heavens. It came from the direction whence winter comes and it moved toward the lake, passing over the church. The ball of fire measured some 140 feet from one edge to the other and over the same distance, ahead of it, two ardent rays were extended.

That was not the end of the sighting, however, for the extraordinary object came back twice:

> Less than an hour later, it suddenly reappeared over the same lake. It darted from the south to the west and it must have been 1,500 feet away when it disappeared. But it came back again, to the great terror of all those who watched it, moving to the west and remaining over Roboziero for an hour and a half.
>
> Fishermen who were in their boat on the lake, a little over one mile away, were deeply burned by the heat. The waters of the lake were illuminated to their greatest depth of thirty feet and the fish swam away toward shore. The water seemed to be covered with rust under the reddish light.[32]

The prudent author of the report took pains to send an investigator, as he concludes:

> And I, your servant, dispatched a messenger to the priests of the district of Bieloziero who confirmed in writing that what was related did happen at that date and place.

The modern public and many researchers often assume that such old reports should be discounted either because people didn't know how to keep proper records or because what they saw must have been tainted with fantastic ideas. In the words of an American ufologist, all that is "folklore of dubious authenticity." Such arguments are used to support the idea that the UFO phenomenon is of recent origin and follows the narrow patterns ascribed to it by the ufologists in question. We have already seen this flawed reasoning at work in the Voronezh case.

The Roboziero report gives the lie to such a hasty judgment. Not only is it one of the earliest cases on record involving beams causing physiological effects, but it is given with all the earmarks of careful investigation and intellectual integrity. It is noteworthy that the people involved, including the author of the report, thought they were preserving the record of a sign from God. They were transmitting it to the highest authority of their church, and the penalties for distortion would have been severe. What we have here is a valuable report from the depth of tsarist Russia, describing the UFO phenomenon in its full glory with its most modern characteristics.

THE HARDCORE DATA

Now we come to the contemporary data. They are contained in files as extensive and as well documented as the Western ones, although it is only in the last twenty years—and at their own perils—that Soviet researchers have analyzed them.

The first scientist who made an effort to compile these observations was Felix Zigel. The result was impressive, not only for the number but for the caliber of the sightings.[33]

According to Zigel, on the morning of April 27, 1961, twenty-five witnesses in the region of Lake Onega, northeast of Leningrad, saw a bluish green oval object the size of a jetliner flying east silently at very high speed. It reportedly came so low that it scraped the ground but flew up again. In the process, it broke the ice on the lake and left a trench fifty feet long and ten feet deep. Sample pieces of the ice, when melted, left a residue of magnesium, aluminum, calcium, barium, and titanium.

A strange piece of metal and tiny black grains, resistant to acid and heat, were also picked up. They were composed of iron, silicon, sodium, lithium, titanium, and aluminum. A joint civilian-military team investigated the incident.

It was in his study of pilot sightings that Zigel excelled, however. One of the most remarkable stories involved a test pilot named Arkady Apraksin, who was twice forced down by a UFO.

The first incident took place on June 16, 1948. Apraksin was flying a jet at 31,000 feet over the Baskuschak region, north of the Caspian Sea, when he saw an unknown object that was also tracked on radar from the ground. Shaped like a banana, the object was emitting beams of light. Apraksin was ordered to force it down, but when he reached a point six miles from the UFO the beams reportedly opened up like a fan and temporarily blinded him while the electrical systems of the jet failed. He was able to glide to a lower altitude and made a crash landing without major damage.

Approximately a year later, on May 6, 1949, Apraksin was test-flying a new plane when he encountered another object under similar circumstances. This time he was able to land on the banks of the Volga River, twenty-six miles north of Saratov.

Beams of light were also reported in a case involving the crew and passengers of a test flight for the State Scientific Institute for Civil Aviation. The date was December 3, 1967, and the plane was at 2,700 feet altitude in the region of Cape Kamenny when an intensely luminous object began following them. Witnesses saw the object for ten minutes before it flew away.

Other Soviet cases were reminiscent of the French wave of sightings in 1954, with elongated objects being observed generating smaller craft.

On September 19, 1968, at 8:00 P.M., an astronomer named Ludmila S. Tsekhanovich saw a bright, pulsating orange ball over the town of Gagra, on the Black Sea. The object came down rapidly and hovered. Tsekhanovich's report continues:

> About thirty seconds later a tiny orange ball appeared and circled the larger object. Three more balls performed the same maneuver. The larger object became elongated and vanished. A minute later there was a flash of light and all the objects were gone.

Other sightings were made by highly placed scientific experts. For instance, on July 31, 1969, L. I. Kupriyanov, doctor of technical sciences, was driving near Usovo (a small town near Moscow) with some of his friends at about 8:00 P.M. when they saw two silver disks flying over them. All the cars in the area stalled.

The sightings continued year after year until the sudden increase recorded in 1989 attracted international attention. The major wave that affected the USSR became a concern to military authorities. On March 21, 1990, radar stations and aircraft were placed on alert when an object was detected in the area of Perslavl-Zaleski near Moscow. A pilot, Lieutenant Colonel A. A. Semenchenko, saw the object, described as "two flashing white lights," at 10:05 P.M.

> The target did not respond to the identify-friend-or-foe request. I approached the target to a range of 1,500 feet. I passed above the target. . . .

General Igor Maltsev, the chief of staff of Soviet Air Defense Forces, published his analysis of the data, based on pilot and radar reports such as the above. Observing that "the UFO hovered above the ground and then flew with a speed exceeding that of modern jet fighters by two or three times," he concluded: "At the present time, terrestrial machines could hardly have any such capabilities."[34]

The secret chronicles of Soviet UFO data are finally becoming part of the public record. Through the efforts of research groups such as those we met during our trip, a rich harvest of observations may be brought to the attention of the world scientific community in all its bewildering diversity.

CHAPTER 13

THE PERM EXPEDITIONS

> While walking along Serginskaya Street at 8:50 P.M. in the city of Perm, my wife, my son, and I observed a strange object in the shape of a ring flying across the sky. We observed it for ten to fifteen minutes. . . .
>
> *Witness Y. G. Solovyev*
> *Perm, August 5, 1967*

The day began with a little crisis. Not only was there no coffee available in the hotel, but there was not even any breakfast! The little counter at the end of our corridor had its iron curtain drawn shut, and the tables were devoid of customers. It was hard enough to get up every morning to face the cold and the jet lag, but doing it on an empty stomach was not an attractive prospect. We started aggressively exploring the huge building in search of food. Downstairs in the big lobby we overheard two burly fellows who spoke English with an American accent, walking around as if they owned the place. They had chains around their necks with U.S.-style security badges dangling from them. The badges were labeled KREMLIN. They looked for all the world like the tough guys in spy movies, except that Western spies rarely carry their identification in such obvious manner when they operate behind the Iron Curtain.

"Do you happen to know where one can get a decent breakfast in this place?" I asked them.

The two shrugged, laughed, argued, and eventually directed us to the fourth floor. Sure enough, we found a little counter there. Behind it three women were serving tea and biscuits and sugary bread. I have even memorized how to ask for butter: *maslo*. But on our way there we had another surprise: we passed an entire row of rooms and offices furnished in Western style. The doors were open and we could see piles of television equipment, cartons of food, and coffee machines that emitted a wonderful odor. We had just discovered the permanent Moscow bureau of ABC News; their offices occupied an entire wing on that floor.

We settled down for breakfast, after which we met our guide Serge, who was looking everywhere for us. He rushed us to a waiting car, explaining that we were late for our meeting with the investigator from Perm.

Mining engineer Emil Bachurin, vice-president of the Perm UFO research group, turned out to be a solid fellow in his early forties with considerable experience in mineral exploration. He had come to Moscow to meet with us, bringing a surprise for me: a copy of his book *Commentaries on "Passport to Magonia."*[35] Written in 1988, it circulated among Soviet ufologists in samizdat form.

Located in the Urals nearly a thousand miles east of Moscow, the Perm region is a heavily frequented zone where UFOs, globes of light, and weird electrical phenomena have been reported for decades. A dedicated researcher with advanced training in geology, Bachurin had taken a scientific approach to the systematic analysis of these cases, no matter how strange. And some of them, as we shall see, were very strange indeed.

CONTACTS AND ABDUCTIONS

On the night of February 6, 1989, a fifty-two-year-old woman who managed a service station in Perm saw a bright disk in the sky. She had gone out to feed her dog when she observed the object just above her. She remembers wishing it would come closer. The disk became very bright and everything turned to confusion for her. All she could recall later was that her dog had bitten her, forcing her to move under the roof overhang, where she was shielded from the light.

Under hypnosis a week later, she stated that two tall silhouettes had been visible in the intense light, but she was unable to provide any other details.

"Biolocation techniques were used," said Bachurin with the casual tone we had now come to expect from Soviet ufologists, who spoke about their dowsing device as if it were as common—and as reliable—as a compass or a voltmeter. "We also measured the field with a quartz oscillator. We reconstructed the process of the contact. The beings had touched the back of her head with a very cold metallic triangle, blocking her memory. She went into the craft with them and was told she would be unable to remember. Now she suffers from migraine headaches, and she often feels that her consciousness is leaving her body."

This particular case launched us into a debate about

claims of abduction and about their interpretation by ufologists both in the West and in the East. About ten years ago, American researchers began taking all claims of abduction at face value, arguing that they were the ultimate proof of extraterrestrial visitation. Although untrained in psychiatry and in the formal use of hypnosis, many started relying on revelations made under trance to support their model of the phenomenon. Anyone voicing concern about such abuse of hypnosis, as I did, was attacked with a vehemence that betrayed considerable inner rage in these researchers, as well as an almost religious passion that made intelligent debate impossible. When I challenged the application of the same technique in the Soviet Union, the reactions were more rational and considerably more polite. Nonetheless, it became clear that many Soviet ufologists were just as willing as their American counterparts to believe in the first-level interpretation of what the witnesses were telling them.

There were significant differences between the approaches taken in the Soviet Union and the United States, however. The Soviets knew more about parapsychology and were willing to temper their conclusions. Furthermore, they did not censor from their data base the observations that failed to fit their theory, no matter how strange.

WHEN ALIENS STEAL FOOD

In part of his manuscript, Bachurin comments on my observation that UFO entities often behave in a way that is reminiscent of the beings of legend, the fairies, sylphs, elves, and leprechauns of medieval chronicles. In particular, he brings up the point (familiar to all folklore students) of the beings who take food from humans.

The incident he relates took place in the city of Ulyanovsk in 1986, and comes from the files of the Commission on Anomalous Phenomena. The witness is a Mr. N., who asked that his name be withheld. One morning, when his wife and child had left the house and he was about to leave for work himself, someone rang the doorbell. Assuming it was simply his wife who had forgotten something, he opened the door. He was astonished to be confronted by a man, some seven feet tall, wearing silver overalls and boots. The intruder declared he was an alien and needed food. Mr. N. was so shocked that without any questions or objections he took his guest to the kitchen and started packing some groceries for him.

As he was now late for work, he mentioned this to the visitor, who answered "I understand" in a Russian spoken with a marked accent, in a low, hoarse voice. Mr. N. locked the door and the two left the house together, the alleged alien carrying the groceries wrapped in old newspapers.

When Mr. N. got on the bus that took him to work, the strange visitor was nowhere to be seen. All day long the witness felt anxious and disturbed. Something urged him to return home as soon as possible, and the feeling became so strong that he found an excuse to leave early.

As soon as he unlocked the front door, he ran to the kitchen, where he discovered that the remaining food had been taken. There were empty paper bags, packages, and wrappings everywhere. There were grains of rice, millet, and salt in the cracks in the floor. The refrigerator and the closets were empty. But if the visitor was the culprit, why had he needed to unwrap everything?

Mr. N. faced another serious problem when his wife came home and naturally demanded to know what had happened to their precious food reserve. At first he tried to make up a story, but he soon had to talk about the visitor in silver boots. Understandably, his wife thought the whole episode was absurd. A terrible scandal followed and the couple came close to a divorce, a situation that is common in the aftermath of close encounters.

PSYCHIC PHENOMENA

Our discussion with Emil Bachurin next turned to the subject of his own observations.

"My experiences began in April 1986," Bachurin told us. "I had been preparing an expedition into the zone where the sightings were most heavily concentrated. People were seeing small globes of light, a few inches to a few feet in diameter, as well as larger craft. There was considerable speculation that a terrestrial base existed in the region."

Several such expeditions have been organized in the remote, forested area near Perm, we learned in the course of the conversation. They were conducted by a dozen different groups coming from all over the country. The results were uneven, Bachurin told us with frankness. Some groups saw nothing and went away disappointed. Others brought back extraordinary stories and even some puzzling photographs. As early as October 1983, Bachurin had spent two nights in the taiga at a spot where snow had been melted by an alleged UFO nearly two hundred feet in diameter, on the borderline of the Perm and Sverdlovsk provinces. In December 1986, his group presented a report on medical examination of close encounter witnesses, including changes in their blood pressure.

"The first contact I had was very negative," Bachurin went on.

"What did you see?" asked Martine, intent on pursuing an interview with someone who claimed to have seen the beings themselves.

"I met two humanoids near my house," he answered matter-of-factly. "The information I received was that I must stop my research and disband the expedition."

"What did they look like? Can you give us a picture?"

Bachurin took the notebook I offered him and produced a sketch of the humanoids, explaining as he drew. "They had gray eyes, only slightly larger than human eyes. They were about five feet tall and wore caps and a jacket with a zipper in front. They had short gray hair. Their hands reached below their knees."

"How many fingers?"

"They had normal hands with five fingers." And then he added as an afterthought: "They also had some scars on their hands."

Well, I thought, here is another case the American abductionists would quickly sweep under the carpet for fear of tainting their fine database of dwarfish, bald entities with huge black eyes.

"How did you know they weren't simply human beings with abnormally long arms?"

Bachurin did not take offense at the inquisitive tone of our probing questions. "One of them followed me," he answered with a shrug. "Evidently he had been in the street for a long time. I felt the psychic intensity that emanated from him. I made a strong effort to hide my own thoughts. All of us in the expedition had trained ourselves in psychotronics. Eventually I took the bus, and the being in question stayed behind. But there were other manifestations. Poltergeists started around the house. Electrical systems blew up; there were short circuits and other problems. Some light bulbs had to be replaced several times a day. The transformer of the television set burned out at a time when the device was not even plugged in."

Bachurin lit a cigarette and went on. "The same day that I saw this being there were several bizarre events. The bus I had taken broke down. We were transferred to another vehicle that got into an accident, so that I ended up going to work on foot! It was like a nightmare. Then, in the evening, I was nearly hit by a car that started rolling down the hill by itself and ended up in someone's backyard. The driver ran after it. I spoke with the man. He swore that the handbrake had been on and the doors were locked."

"Was there any time interval for which you had no recollection that day?"

"No. I got to work on time and my memory of the day is fine, but there is another case when my recollection of events may have been tampered with. It happened in June 1987. Around that time I had a lot of problems with the phone whenever I tried to call other UFO researchers, either no dial tone or just a lot of noise on the line. Then someone, a neighbor of mine, saw a strange being in the garden behind my house. I was not home at the time. The being looked like it was dressed in a diving suit. The neighbor called my wife and asked, 'When did Emil decide to become a frogman?' The being had a skintight outfit and a helmet. Our house is less than three quarters of a mile away from the river, but there was no reason for someone with a diving suit to be there."

"What kind of investigation was done?"

"We used biolocation and found an anomaly at that spot, but hypnosis of my neighbor led nowhere. He simply remembered seeing the frogman in my garden. The whole episode was absurd, yet it happened. And that is typical of the sightings in the Perm region."

The kind of absurdity to which Bachurin referred has been a characteristic of the phenomenon for a long time. French researcher Aimé Michel first noticed it during the 1954 wave in France, when he spoke of "a festival of absurdities."

THE BLACK HAND MYSTERY

In *Commentaries on "Passport to Magonia,"* Bachurin returns to the topic of abductions several times. One of the most remarkable episodes has to do with an incident in which the abducting entity remained largely invisible, except for its arms, which looked human and were black.

Readers of *Magonia* and of my recent book *Dimensions* may recall an encounter that happened on the banks of the Loire River in 1950, in which a young woman was grabbed by two black hands that came literally out of thin air and dragged her through fields and bushes, eventually dropping her. She staggered to a police station, where her injuries (consisting mainly of cuts and bruises and understandable shock) were verified.

The case was first published in the journal *Lumières dans la Nuit* in January 1967. It was later picked up in an article by Gordon Creighton in the February 1978 issue of the British journal *Flying Saucer Review* titled "A French Parallel to the Vila Velha Attempted Abduction."

I have often discussed the case with Gordon Creighton, and we both remarked that it seemed to represent an exception in the patterns of reported abductions. Now Emil Bachurin has given us yet another such exception.

The incident happened in a remote part of the woods in Gorky Province and was related to Bachurin by V. V. Proshin, a member of the local section of the Commission on Anomalous Phenomena. The case concerned the daughter of a forester who, one warm summer evening, was quietly sitting on a windowsill, with her back to the open window. Suddenly, two black hands grabbed her waist and tried to drag her out the open window. The girl shouted in fear and managed to hold on to the window frame. She turned her head and looked back. She saw that she was held by "arms alone" that became "vague, diffuse" in the places where they were supposed to be attached to the body.

It was still fairly light. In the yard, the dog howled wildly and rushed toward the window.

The hands let go of the girl, and she nearly fainted. Her father, who had been alerted by her screams, ran outside with his gun in his hand. The dog was barking at empty space in front of the window. There was no one in sight.

This extraordinary Soviet sighting, which corroborates the 1950 Loire River incident, sent me back on a search of older records. I found yet another "black hand" case, this time in a rare book of demonology published in 1854 entitled *Moeurs et Pratiques des Demons ou des Esprits Visiteurs* by Gougenot des Mousseaux. Describing a series of unexplained manifestations that took place in Cideville, Normandy, circa 1850, the author relates a number of apparent encounters with invisible entities. He wrote, "One day one of the two children sees a black hand that comes close to him and strikes him."

Such incidents, in my view, throw a completely new light on the abduction reports that have too long been treated in a purely extraterrestrial context.

GLOBES OF LIGHT AND ENERGY FIELDS

The various expeditions that attempted to clarify and document the Perm observations have brought back no proof, but they did generate interesting reports and a few photographs deserving of analysis. We reviewed this data with Emil Bachurin and Alexis Konin, a Novosti journalist who had taken a personal interest in the region and who had been a member of a recent winter expedition there.

Some of the photographs (reproduced in the picture section of this book) show small spheres of light hovering a few feet off the ground. We wondered if these phenomena could be explained as photographic artifacts, especially in view of the extreme cold that was in evidence at the time.

Freezing weather produces a whole range of effects on emulsions, from condensation to small tears of the film. We were assured that precautions had been taken against such effects and that witnesses at the site had actually seen the globes of light when the pictures were taken, so for the time being they have to be regarded as unexplained.

In other cases, the phenomena were indeed easy to identify. For instance, we were shown pictures of alleged "energy fields" that were clearly related to a fine but ordinary display of the northern lights. The Perm region is located far enough to the north for the aurora borealis to be a common sight, one with which I would have expected the Soviet ufologists to be completely familiar.[36] To the trained eye, one of these pictures showed the Big Dipper with star trails clearly indicating a time exposure, with a typical auroral pattern below.

Are the globes of light seen in Perm evidence of an undiscovered natural effect rather than a manifestation of an intelligence? Some researchers in the West, notably U.S. geologist Dr. John Derr and British author Paul Devereux, have argued that physical stresses within the earth could generate luminous objects that might be mistaken for UFOs. Devereux even went beyond this hypothesis when he suggested that "earth lights," as he called them, might themselves be endowed with a form of consciousness.[37]

"How long has this region been a focus for such reports?" I asked Bachurin.

"We really don't know," he said. "But some of the recent observations were made at the sacred site of Moliobka, which an ancient people already regarded as endowed by divine energy. The Mansi had actually erected a monument there." (The Mansi are a Finno-Ugric people, one of many minority groups in the Soviet Union.) Bachurin added: "I read in one of your books about the case of Maurice Masse in Valensole.

He experienced so much sleepiness after his encounter that he could not stay awake for even four hours. Well, during one of my own experiences in October 1987, I was exposed to a peculiar form of light, about 3:00 A.M., and I fell asleep almost instantly. I had a gun in my hands and I had just shouted 'Halt! Who is there?' when the light hit me."

In the Perm region, as in other parts of the world, it is clear that the phenomenon is not a new development. The challenge before researchers in both the East and the West is to study the characteristics of the sightings and to analyze carefully the resulting patterns. There is considerable disagreement among scientists about their meaning, as we would find out in our next series of conversations.

CHAPTER 14

THE VIEW FROM ACADEME

One of my coworkers at the astronomical observatory invited me to watch a UFO. Naturally, I didn't believe him but, as he put it, a witness was necessary and I was it. . . .

We climbed on the roof of the refractor and began to look toward the northwest. At approximately 5:15 P.M. in the area of Alpha of Corona Borealis a half moon appeared, moving through the sky. . . .

Astronomer Y. L. Chikanov
Kazan, November 7, 1967

There are no miracles. There is no reason for all this commotion. In the Soviet Union more than two hundred artificial earth satellites have been launched. This activity is even more widely organized in the United States. And thousands of balloons are sent up to determine the temperature of the upper atmosphere. There are no new phenomena.

V. I. Krasovsky,
doctor of physical and mathematical sciences
Moscow, February 5, 1968

It was in a very modern, even plush meeting room of Novosti that we were formally introduced to Professor Vladimir Migulin, member of the Soviet Academy of Sciences, who held the chair of physical sciences of vibrations (also known as radiophysics) at the University of Moscow.

A polite, distinguished physicist in his sixties, Professor Migulin saluted us stiffly. We took our seats with our interpreters in a circle of leather chairs, while secretaries brought us the customary tea in exquisite cups of fine china. We drained the cups as Professor Migulin, who reminded me of Donald Menzel, proceeded to explain to us why unidentified flying objects could not possibly exist, in spite of numerous sightings reported by scientists all over the country.

EVOLUTION OF A DEBATE

In any review of the history of the UFO phenomenon in the Soviet Union, it is apparent that the controversy follows lines that are a close parallel to the evolving situation in the West. Thus it should not come as a surprise that most Soviet scientists, like their American counterparts, are still skeptical of the reality of the phenomenon. The quotes by Artsimovich, Krasovsky, and others that we have used in earlier chapters to illustrate the debate show that opposition to the study of UFOs was as fierce and strident in the East as it was in the West. While it is generally true that those professional scientists who have taken the trouble to investigate the sightings themselves usually end up fascinated by the phenomenon, there are exceptions to this rule. Vladimir Migulin is such an exception, as he made very clear to us.

"I began this study in the 1960s when Alexandrov, the president of the Academy of Sciences, asked me to monitor the reports and to try to explain them within the scope of known physical laws."

In other words, Migulin's mission was close to that assigned to Dr. J. Allen Hynek by the U.S. Air Force, but the former acted very discreetly indeed. Dr. Hynek certainly had no idea that he had such a counterpart in the USSR, and to my knowledge they were never in contact. (Hynek, of course, was aware of Felix Zigel and Alexander Kazantsev after my visit in 1966.) While Hynek's views on the subject changed over the years, Migulin is just as much a skeptic today as he was at the beginning.

"I have been working on this problem with Dr. Platov and with other specialists of terrestrial magnetism," continued Migulin. "I also served as a deputy to the academy's secretary for physics and astronomy, who is one of the discoverers of the principle of the laser. He has no interest in the UFO phenomenon. I do, but only out of duty, because I have been assigned this job."

That's an old story, I reflected. The scientists who have been given an official mission to study these sightings have generally been people like Migulin who had no personal motivation to do the work. Those who had both the skills and the passion for this research were never given the means to pursue it. We will never know what they might have discovered.

If the church had confiscated Galileo's telescope, turning it over to a committee of so-called unbiased cardinals appointed by the pope, would the phases of Venus, the satellites of Jupiter, and the reality of sunspots ever have been discovered?

"The sightings can be explained by a variety of causes," said Migulin. "We have to keep in mind that the effects, the reports, are one thing, and the phenomenon is quite another. Some of the effects are manmade. For instance, people have described some fantastic things in the sky in Petrosovotsk, near Lake Onega, north of Moscow; they saw a large light shaped like a medusa, and an object flying from south to north. Well, it turned out to be a secret rocket launch; the real explanation had not been released."

The reader may recall that in Chapter 7 we mentioned the important article that Migulin and Platov had published in January 1979, inviting the population to report UFO sightings to the Academy of Sciences. Clearly, the results had not led to any dramatic reassessment.

"Granted that many of the reports are explainable," I said to Migulin, "how do you deal with those that still remain unidentified?"

"That is a very small number. Ninety or ninety-five percent of our reports are explainable. Of course, some of our scientists disagree with that. Recently a group has been formed around Vlail Kaznacheyev, a medical researcher in Siberia. But our academy considers this a waste of time. Kaznacheyev believes in extraterrestrials."

"So what do you do with the reports that are not explainable? Doesn't that reveal a genuine problem?"

Migulin dismissed the question with a wave of his hand. "I don't deny that we are unable to account for some of the observations. That is perfectly natural. There are always cases where information is so obsolete, insufficient, contradictory, confusing, or emotional that we cannot find the explanation. In such cases we know that some sort of phenomenon has taken place, but people have probably misinterpreted it. Very often human imagination is at the root of the problem. Besides," he added with heavy irony, "no extraterrestrials have ever shown up on photographs."

Those were arguments I had not heard in the West for many years. It is now a well-demonstrated fact that the unexplained reports often contain more data, with greater precision and reliability than the identified cases. In fact, that observation represents the real challenge of the UFO problem. If the data were always "obsolete, insufficient, contradictory," the problem would have gone away a long time ago.

As for the lack of pictures of extraterrestrials, that represents another example of faulty reasoning. Why should UFOs, if they exist, necessarily be extraterrestrial in nature?

I gathered up my courage and challenged the academician. "You know, Professor Migulin, in the Middle Ages people used to describe strange and terrible phenomena in the sky, such as bloody swords held by the hand of God. We even have engravings that show such effects. The scientists of that day could well have argued, as you do, that the reports were too emotional and contradictory to be taken seriously. Instead they were open-minded enough to preserve the information. If they had destroyed it we might have missed some important records of ancient comets. Today we know that comets are not swords held in the sky by the hand of God, of course; we can separate what people *think* they saw from the real phenomenon. Why not apply the same open-minded approach to UFOs?

"What we have here is an unexplained phenomenon of massive proportion. Shouldn't we try to document it and to analyze it? The fact that the public and the believers have already jumped to the conclusion that it must be caused by extraterrestrials may be aberration, of course, just like the hand of God holding the sword, but that should not stop us from doing our job as scientists."

Migulin may have felt the weight of these arguments, because he replied to me without acrimony. "I am familiar with your opinion, and I have read the works of Hynek and Menzel in this field. But the idea that some form of consciousness is manifested by the UFO phenomenon is only a hypothesis, one that has never been proven. We cannot expect to discover any new law in this regard, at least before the end of the century."

Up to that point our debate, although tense, had been kept cool and considerate, with the mutual respect that is customary among scientists. Who was I to give a lesson in scientific methodology to a Soviet academician, and in his own country, too? For Migulin's part, he remained a courteous host, although it was obvious that we had a fundamental disagreement.

But an unexpected new factor suddenly appeared in our group. The three Novosti interpreters who were with us stopped doing the translation to jump squarely into the debate.

"What about the cases from the latest wave?" one of them asked angrily. "How about the pictures taken in the Perm region, in full daylight, Professor? How can you say that the sightings there are explainable by conservative physics, relying on well-known laws of nature?"

Martine and I watched the scene with some amazement. Later we reflected that it reminded us of the confrontations between French students and the older bosses of the French academic structure during the turbulent period of May 1968. It was very obvious that Professor Vladimir Migulin, holder of the chair of radiophysics at Moscow University and a full member of the prestigious Academy of Sciences of the USSR, was not used to being pushed around by a bunch of youngsters. It was a new experience for him and he did not like it.

"Why won't scientists study this?" asked one of the Novosti men, spreading photographs over the table.

"Scientists don't have anything to work with here. Science can only operate on verified facts."

"Have you discussed this with Kaznacheyev?"

"I already told you: we think he is wasting his time."

"Have you looked at Azhazha's data?"

Migulin shrugged and replied. "I've known him for ten years. He only plays a positive role in this debate to the extent that he contributes new data. But his sources are not reliable."

"What about the observations at Voronezh?"

"I didn't go there myself, so I don't want to say too much about it. The witnesses make all sorts of claims that sound like hoaxes to me. These people may be mentally ill, you know. Or else they are lying. The phenomenon they describe has been linked to a rocket launch from Volgograd, on a second-by-second basis. It has all been explained."

The alleged explanation did not hold, of course. There were numerous low-level observations at Voronezh over a two-week period, and there were ground traces in the park. They could not be accounted for by simple rocket firings.

The conversation had taken an aggressive turn. It was conducted in rapid volleys exchanged in Russian, so that my record of it is woefully incomplete. The outcome was clear, however: the argument, predictably, had left everyone on his position.

It was Martine who brought the discussion back to a temperate level. "The other evening," she said, "Alexander Kazantsev told us of an object with a very curious composition. It seemed to have crashed near the Varta River in 1975. Have you investigated this incident?"

"I have heard of the case, but I am not as impressed with it as Kazantsev is. I think what we have here is simply a combination of terrestrial materials."

Martine pressed on politely. "But it seems to have been manufactured in outer space, Professor."

"Perhaps it was," said Migulin with a smile. "What is so surprising about that? We are conducting advanced metallurgical experiments in orbit."

"Why would they have dropped pieces of that metal? Surely it would be very valuable if it was manufactured aboard *Soyuz* or *Salyut*."

The academician was obviously reluctant to answer the question.

"What about the new research group headed by Vladimir Azhazha?" asked Martine, turning to a new topic. "Isn't that a valuable step in the study?"

"He doesn't have a state budget," said Migulin. "He hopes to get some funds, but for the moment his work is purely private."

I joined in at that point. "What about the Soviet military? There are numerous indications that they have conducted their own studies."

"Yes, they have," he conceded. "Some fifteen years ago our armed forces set up a research group that collaborated with the academy. But it was abolished five years later for lack of results."

Perhaps I should have brought up the Cuban case, but I had the distinct feeling that the debate had been pushed as far as it could be.

"It is the human factor, the psychology of the witnesses, that plays the greatest role," concluded Migulin, implying again that the unexplained cases were the product of overheated imagination. He added in a conciliatory way: "We must continue to look at the problem. We have to wait for new facts."

I changed the subject again. "During this trip we have heard a lot of surprising comments about biolocation. What do you think of that phenomenon?"

I fully expected that Migulin would treat dowsing with the same contempt he had shown for UFO data. In the West the American Association for the Advancement of Science long denied membership to the very scholarly Parapsychological Association because it did research on such forbidden topics. (The AAAS only accepted it in 1969.) In France Professor Yves Rocard, one of the most influential physicists under Charles de Gaulle and father of a socialist prime minister, had failed to be elected to the Academy of Sciences because he dared to set up an experiment to test dowsing ability and to publish the results. Here again, however, Migulin had a surprise for us.

"Biolocation must be seriously studied," he said flatly. "I do not have a personal hypothesis to explain it, but you should expect some breakthroughs from the biological standpoint."

"So you would agree that the effect is real?"

"I don't deny it. There are many such effects that cannot be explained by modern science. Hypnosis, for instance. Biolocation may belong in the same category. Of course it is difficult for science to study such phenomena unless they are reproducible with good reliability."

"So . . . should we take your answer to mean that you are looking for a scientific explanation in terms of classical effects?"

"Yes, all we can say is that biolocation represents the interaction of biological objects with the environment. Again, I don't have a personal hypothesis to offer. We are studying the effects of electric and magnetic fields on these abilities. Many more experiments are needed."

Professor Migulin looked at his watch. We understood that the interview was at an end. Handshakes were exchanged. We were left with the feeling that the view from academe was a very complex and subtle one indeed, even if many of the answers given to the public were of the standard debunking type. Something was going on under the surface; between the lines of our dialogue there was evidence of official concern and of a powerful controversy ready to erupt.

We would have a clear confirmation of it the very next day.

CHAPTER 15

TURNING A PAGE IN THE BOOK OF SCIENCE

The problem of UFOs has captured the attention of the public and of many scientists. For a long time, some of them have asserted that there are no such phenomena in nature and that reports about them were caused either by optical illusions or by careless observations.

Recently, however, it has become impossible to hold such a view. UFOs continue to be observed, not by chance witnesses who do not inspire confidence, but by professional astronomers and other scientists and by pilots.

It serves no purpose for us to refrain from public scientific investigations in this field.

Dr. M. M. Protodyakonov,
deputy director of the Earth Sciences Institute, Soviet Academy of Sciences
Major General G. A. Uger (Ret.),
editor in chief of Foreign Electronics Magazine
L. M. Leonov, writer
V. I. Borbunov, aircraft designer
Col. G. F. Sivakov, Air Force Engineering Academy
Dr. Y. V. Ryabov,
dean of the Military Engineering Academy

It was partially to repay the hospitality of our hosts, and partially to launch a wider debate that I hoped to pursue in future years, that I suggested the idea of a friendly roundtable with local ufologists. What I had in mind was an informal, American-style exchange during which we could review some of the theories about UFOs, their history, the structure of the phenomenon, and its possible meaning.

"Very good idea," our Novosti friends had said. "On Friday we will organize such a roundtable, as you say, with a few researchers from Moscow. Then, in the afternoon, why don't you plan to give a more general lecture for the press?"

What they did not tell me was that there was no such thing as an American-style roundtable in Russia. Perhaps there had been a mistake in the translation. But our informal seminar, as it turned out, would initiate one of the more significant scientific debates I had ever attended on the subject. The evening lecture also turned into a formal symposium in front of four hundred journalists. At the end of the day our understanding of the phenomenon in general, and its impact in the Soviet Union in particular, had been further shattered.

Any illusion that we would be spending the morning in an informal exchange was quickly left behind when we entered the large rectangular room where the meeting was scheduled to take place. There were microphones everywhere, booths manned by interpreters at one end, a bust of Lenin at the other, and some twenty-five participants in suits and ties seated at the huge conference table, pens and paper before them, tape recorders at the ready. Vladimir Azhazha and I were given seats under a portrait of Mikhail Gorbachev, and Vice-Chairman Milyutenko gave us a friendly but thoroughly serious introduction, after which we each had the floor for half an hour. A general discussion followed.

The tone of that discussion was given by the first speaker, who introduced himself as the head of an important physical laboratory of the Academy of Sciences. His interest, predictably, was landing traces. He had been studying them for many years. I asked about recent cases.

"We have a catalog of thirty landings recorded between August and November 1989," he answered, "in the single region of Nicolayev near the Black Sea. The folks in Voronezh are not the only ones who have reported such phenomena."

It was a theme that would recur during the whole discussion: Voronezh was far from an isolated incident. It wasn't even terribly significant. There were better data around. And they had been analyzed in the field and in the laboratory by teams of scientists.

This was the story the Western press had missed.

Other people introduced themselves listing their degrees, their affiliations, their years of experience with UFOs. A new realization started sinking into my mind: it would not be easy to bring together a similar group in the United States, or in Western Europe. Many scientists who once belonged to specialized UFO organizations have deserted them in the last few years, driven away by dogmatic gurus who tried to impose their own theories, or disgusted by the pointless fights between the abductionists and the conspiracy believers. The leaders of these organizations only welcomed within their ranks those scientists who agreed with them, without realizing that it is basic to the training of a real scientist to challenge *all* preconceived notions, including his own. As a result, field investigations had fallen to a very low point in the West. Why bother to analyze traces, to compile accurate databases, or to look for patterns if one could simply force the White House, Congress, the Pentagon, or some other group to reveal the truth they surely possess? Why go through the hard work of checking the accuracy of the reports and the reliability of witnesses when the full nature of the phenomenon will surely be disclosed by the next abductee we hypnotize?

While American ufologists fell into this trap, Soviet researchers have managed to avoid it until now. Perhaps that is only a temporary situation: the temptation will be great to rush into the same sort of activity. We have already seen how hypnosis was used in the USSR in combination with such unproven techniques as biolocation. But the Soviets' passion for a complete research framework and their experience with parapsychology has allowed them to preserve a sane perspective.

Questions fused around the table. Many people were curious about the role played by the debunker Donald Menzel. What about all the rumors of a secret study? Were parapsychological techniques used in connection with UFO investigations? Were we aware of the religious implications? Were there ongoing anthropological or ethnological studies of the UFO phenomenon? Had the United States and France conducted research on the microbiology of UFO landing sites and if not, why not? To some of these questions I felt I could give adequate answers. Others left me forced to confess ignorance. I could see that the people around the table were surprised to hear that in the West such research was left to individual scientists working with their own resources.

One of the specialists said he belonged to a scientific interdisciplinary center that was a technical collective with a new methodology. The focus of the center's research was on contactees and abductees. The group had developed two complementary techniques to interview and test them. Researchers were aware of the many pitfalls of hypnosis, and they were very careful not to lead or influence the witnesses in any way.

When I brought up five arguments I had developed that conflicted with the extraterrestrial hypothesis (these arguments have to do with the abnormally high frequency of close encounters, the long history of the sightings, the shape and behavior of the occupants and the ability of the objects to change shape dynamically), the discussion group seemed to split into two factions. The first side held firmly to the ETH, arguing that it was the only theory that could explain craft coming from the sky. One person said that he could produce counterarguments to all five of the points I had raised. I told him truthfully that I would welcome such a debate: it's about time such questions be put on the table.

The second group had no problem whatsoever with alternatives to the extraterrestrial theory. They quoted Konstantin Tsiolkovsky, pointing out that the idea of multiple dimensions and parallel universes filled with consciousness was a valid scientific speculation.

"Perhaps the beings described by witnesses are an intermediate lifeform between us and that form of consciousness," one man said. "The various theories are not mutually exclusive."

This is an appropriate place to pay special tribute to Konstantin Tsiolkovsky (1857–1935), a Polish émigré to Russia who, as early as 1920, had come to the conclusion that the earth was being observed by alien forms of intelligence and was theorizing why they had not openly sought contact with us. A rocket pioneer, Tsiolkovsky gave careful consideration to several theories about such beings. Remarkably, he did not restrict himself to a nuts-and-bolts interpretation, even speculating about esoteric views. "Could advanced beings colonize the ethereal plane around stars?" he asked.

Most important, notes the Estonian researcher Yuri Lina in an unpublished manuscript, Tsiolkovsky proposed the hypothesis that advanced alien societies might already be influencing humanity, in ways unknown to us.

Some of the scientists around the table echoed these views, reminding one another that consciousness and intelligence could take many forms.

"Life could also manifest in the form of energy fields," added another participant.

In Silicon Valley I had heard the same speculation from Dr. Charlie Rosen, a pioneer in robotics. "Think of all the things you could do if you were a superconducting cloud half the size of the solar system," Charlie had said. "UFOs could be just the simplest form of manifestation for such an entity, a shape it might assume to get our attention!"

The Soviets were speculating along similar lines. "There may be undiscovered forms of plasma consciousness in the universe," someone said.

"They could also have evolved right here when the

earth was still in a plasma form," another broke in. "They could have existed on this planet long before mankind appeared."

"We have always assumed that human consciousness was the master force on earth," another participant pointed out. "Perhaps the UFO phenomenon will teach us that we were grossly mistaken."

STATISTICAL ANALYSIS

Whether or not we are the dominant form of consciousness on earth, the Soviets' own statistics show conclusively that the UFO phenomenon is present in all regions of the planet with an identical behavior. In a report published in 1979 by the Academy of Sciences, time and space data were found to correlate closely among Soviet samples and Western databases.[38]

Using as a framework the statistics that Claude Poher and I had published in a report to the American Institute of Aeronautics and Astronautics, the three authors of the Soviet study found that half of all sightings in their sample lasted between one and nineteen minutes, a duration that is clearly adequate for detailed observation.[39] The corresponding figure for reports of such duration was one-third in the French and non-French databases that Poher and I had compiled. Less than 10 percent of the Soviet cases had a duration of less than ten seconds, while approximately one case in three lasted over twenty minutes. These figures, too, showed that the problem presented itself in similar terms all over the world.

The Soviet researchers also verified the Law of the

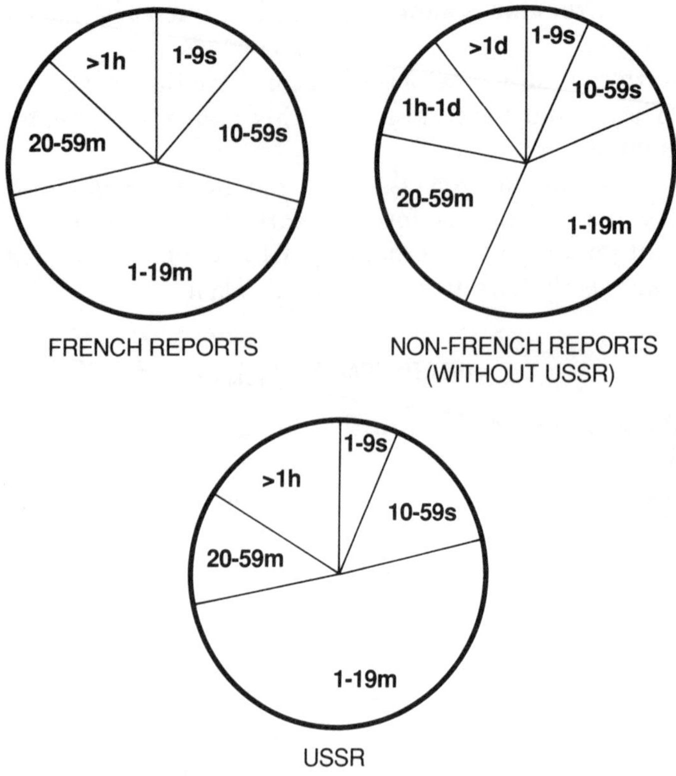

Fig. 8. Distribution of Soviet sightings by duration, in excellent agreement with published patterns from Jacques Vallee and Claude Poher.

Times first noted in my book *Challenge to Science*.[40] According to this pattern, which has now been verified in every major region, sighting frequency tends to increase in the early evening hours, going through a maximum between 9:00 and 10:00 P.M., perhaps because the number of potential witnesses go to bed around that time. What the actual curve would look

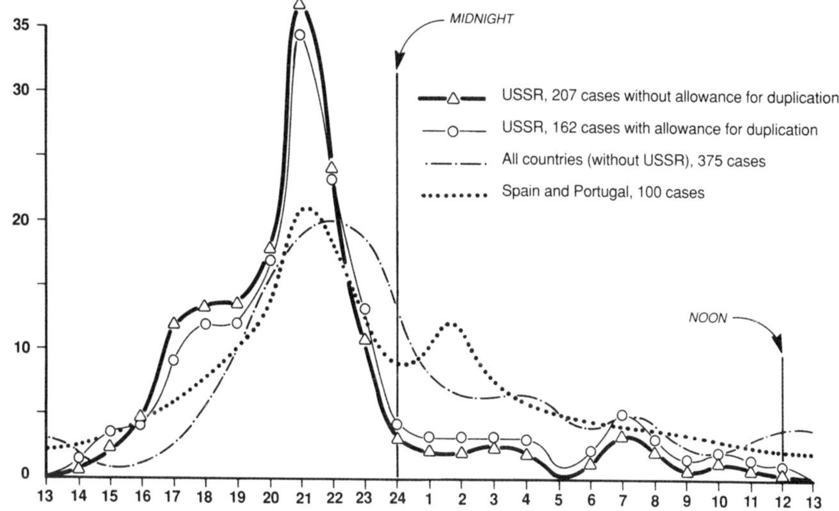

Fig. 9. The Law of the Times in the USSR as compared to the author's database of non-Soviet cases. The confirmation is striking.

like if the population stayed outside during the night is anybody's guess, of course.

Of special interest is the remark made in the report regarding the objects' changes of shapes, which we have noted earlier as a major characteristic of the phenomenon. According to the Soviet scientists:

> These changes include change of shape of the object (transition from one shape to another); separation of one object from another; the connection of one object to another; "extinction" of a luminous object; gradual dissipation of an object; [and] origination of a new object.

It is perhaps in this area that the Soviet students of the phenomenon have been most perceptive, while Western specialists remained obsessed with static models that assumed UFOs to be spacecraft endowed with such things as propulsion systems and a fixed shape. As the Soviet report observes:

> When such changes occur, we speak of several phases of *forming*. In each phase, the objects have a stable shape. Any change means a transition to the next phase. Phases of the phenomenon can be distinguished by other characteristics, for example, by a change in the parameters of motion. In order to emphasize that the matter has to do with changes in shape, we call the corresponding phases "forming phases."

At this point I am not aware of any similar study of shape transitions in the West. The Soviet authors have computed that in over three-quarters of their samples, eyewitnesses observed one forming phase. In 11 percent of the cases two phases were seen, three phases in 8 percent of the cases, and more than three phases in 3.5 percent of the sample. In total, the Soviet catalog contained no less than 149 separate changes or transitions affecting the objects.

It is unfortunate that these statistical studies published ten years ago have not been pursued aggressively, but the same critical remark could be made about the United States. Efforts to maintain such catalogs, even over a limited geographical area, represent a long-term investment of time, energy, and statistical skill that few volunteer organizations can afford. Furthermore, the basic tool of such a catalog, namely, a good, simple, efficient, and mnemonic classification system, has never been available. A new effort in this direction is given here in the appendix, but it is too early to tell if it can be applied successfully to the Soviet data. As a first step, I have given a case index of all the sightings mentioned in this book, with the caveat, of course, that it constitutes only a very small sample of the overall phenomenon in the Soviet Union.

Another aspect of the field with which the Soviet researchers seem perfectly comfortable has to do with the mythological, religious, and anthropological factors. Numerous researchers, like the scientific historian Vladimir Rubtsov in Kharkov and the ethnographer Valeri Sanarov in Novosibirsk, have conducted extensive analyses of this problem. (The latter is the author of an article entitled "UFO and Ufonauts in the Light of Folklore" published in *Technology for Youth*, no. 11, 1979.) During our roundtable discussion several people brought up the point and asked incisive questions about studies being done in the West, and about my own philosophical position on the matter. I had to admit that, with few exceptions (notably in the very popular domain of speculation about ancient astronauts and possible reinterpretations of the Bible), our social scientists had not paid much attention to the phenomenon either in its modern or in its historical aspect. As for the major UFO civilian research organizations in the United States, they had increasingly discouraged this line of research out of a narrow policy that emphasized the abductionist theory and the space visitors concept, almost in a return to the ideas made popular by Major Keyhoe in the mid-fifties. Some Soviet researchers, of course, have also remained faithful to this view. But my impression was that the younger scientists in the groups I met were aggressively moving toward new hypotheses.

When I asked them why they were so interested in the UFO phenomenon, one of them answered very directly. "We want to turn a page in the book of science."

That was a very refreshing statement. In the West a similar group would probably have answered: "We are looking for a breakthrough in propulsion," or "We see an opportunity here to make contact with extraterrestrial intelligence."

Both of these replies are interesting and very valid motivations, but they attack the data at the wrong level. UFOs may not represent extraterrestrial intelligence at all, and they may not use propulsion as we understand it. To look for the propulsion system inside a flying saucer may well be as ludicrous as opening up the hood of a car to find out where the horse is hidden. But any solution to the mystery will necessarily challenge many aspects of our knowledge, and indeed it may turn a page in the book of science.

A PHONE CALL FROM VORONEZH

Over dinner with Vladimir Azhazha and his wife in their Moscow apartment that night, we reviewed the impressions of the day and the lessons of the trip. We also had a chance to discuss in more detail the rapid changes that were taking place in the training and deployment of field investigators in the USSR. Under Azhazha's leadership, an institute had been established where volunteers could take a sixty-hour curriculum covering the methodology and history of UFO research. Over two hundred students had already graduated from the course, we were told.

Halfway through dinner the telephone rang and our host excused himself from the table. He came back with exciting news. "They were calling me from Voronezh," he told us. "They've had another sighting. The object projected beams of light that melted the asphalt before block #5 of the nuclear power plant. There were many witnesses. The Voronezh group took pieces of the asphalt for analysis."

"Professor Migulin told us he thought the sightings in Voronezh were simply mistaken observations of rocket launches from Volgograd," I pointed out.

Azhazha looked at me with surprise. "I am shocked to hear he even suggested such a thing," he said. "All the launches from Volgograd are toward the east. But Voronezh is to the northwest of the rocket site. Besides, how could a rocket flying over Voronezh melt the asphalt in a parking lot?"

MINUS TWENTY-SEVEN

On our last day in Moscow the outside temperature was twenty-seven below zero and still dropping. Our interpreter, Serge, who drove to the airport with us after retrieving our precious passports from the security desk at the Russia Hotel, told us the weather was merely becoming "interesting." The last photographs we took on Red Square show dark, indistinct silhouettes with the gray blur of giant buildings in the background. Serge told us that on July 31, 1982, six unidentified spheres had flown over this celebrated landmark, and in late November 1989, Novosti employees themselves had been able to watch a bright cylindrical object in the sky over the city for fifteen minutes.

Our driver turned on the radio to catch the latest news bulletins. Serge, who listened intently, suddenly began to laugh. "Perhaps you should postpone your departure, my friends," he said. "They have just found an old man who had disappeared for three days in the Ukraine. He says that some alien beings abducted him!"

Clearly, the Russian wave was far from over, I thought, as I looked at the enamel medal representing Tsiolkovsky the organizers of the meeting had presented to me the previous day. There would be many more cases for the scientists to study and for the philosophers to ponder.

CONCLUSION

The well-known Russian scientist Konstantin Tsiolkovsky admitted the possibility that space and time were multidimensional. Moreover, he thought that ethereal beings could live in a parallel dimension to ours.

Journalist O. V. Stolyarov
Voronezh, October 1989

Humanity, without even suspecting it, has attracted the attention of this intelligence and stopped being a self-contained system. Apparently we've tread on the corns of some supercivilization, and it has decided to regulate our progress as it sees fit. *Arkady and Boris Strugatsky*
Definitely Maybe, *1977*

Several months have now passed since we returned from Moscow. In our minds our trip to the Soviet Union has come to assume the features of a dream or a fairy tale. We vaguely remember the frustration and occasional anger, the impossible telephone system, the mornings without breakfast, and the ominous shadows in the corners of the hotel hallways. Indeed, there were difficulties to be overcome at every turn, but those moments of discontent were overwhelmed by magical visions of Blessed Basil's towering bulbs seen through the falling snow, the frozen glint of the icy Moskova River by moonlight, and the hospitality and friendliness of the people we met.

Above all there was the intense feeling of a mystery shared. The words of Vladimir Azhazha stayed with me. We had never met before. Yet he had said, during the very first hour of our dialogue, "It is as if you and I had been working together for the last ten years."

Azhazha and his colleagues had independently noticed that UFO phenomena were polymorphic. They recognized that this was one of the fundamental characteristics of the problem, and this understanding placed them at the forefront of international research. The possibility that UFOs might be an indication of the existence of higher physical dimensions, which is still regarded as a strange notion in the West, has long been present in the minds of Soviet scientists, as the ideas of Konstantin Tsiolkovsky indicate.

Another important factor they acknowledged was the impact that the phenomenon, in its historical form, had undoubtedly had on religious concepts and on social ideas about space. We saw evidence of it in a movie entitled *In Search of the Visitors* that was produced at the Kiev studios in 1988. This film, created under official auspices with the participation of numerous physical and social scientists, including the scientific historian Vladimir Rubtsov, opened up a wide array of hypotheses before the public, and it did so in a sober, academic manner without ever becoming pedantic or boring. We were told it had received wide exposure throughout the Soviet Union both in theatres and on television. It was clear that many trained minds were considering the hypothesis that phenomena like biblical apparitions or the Fatima miracle should be reinterpreted within the mythological framework of the UFO phenomenon. Such speculation, considered marginal at best in the West, and discouraged by many church hierarchies, is becoming a topic of mainstream research among Soviet sociologists.

While we agreed on many aspects of this vast field, there were others on which we had creative disagreements with our Soviet colleagues. For instance, we differed with Larissa Kolessova on her assessment of astrology, and we continued to challenge the authenticity of the UMMO symbol on the side of the Voronezh object. And we were not blind to the fact that many Soviet sightings either were sorely lacking in documentation or came from unreliable sources.

Another point of contention among us was the importance and usefulness of hypnosis in the study of abductees. It seemed to us that hypnotic regression, in many Soviet cases, was conducted with the same lack of standards and precautions that characterized the enthusiastic, but often misguided, American research. Our Soviet friends assured us that they were well aware of the pitfalls of hypnosis, but their whole methodology, in my opinion, has yet to be independently tested. Too often, they have simply swallowed the lies that abound in the Western literature about such topics as abductions and crashed saucers, and adopted them as gospel simply because these stories came from the United States.

The topic of biolocation, which had intrigued us so much that it had initially motivated our trip to Moscow, has remained a tantalizing puzzle. It is not so much the extent to which dowsing was used and applied that surprised us, as it is the high level of reliability Soviet researchers ascribed to it. In the multiple discussions we had we could not see how the experts justified such extensive reliance on this technique, however interesting it might be. Obviously, we still have much to learn in this area.

Finally, we came back from the Soviet Union with a set of unanswered questions about the full extent of the research activity in official institutions. Several incidents, which are outside the scope of this book, suggested that our presence in Moscow was regarded as more than a simple opportunity for an exchange of information on an interesting scientific subject. The high level at which we were greeted, the various personalities to whom we were introduced, and the status of some of the people who attended the various meetings were all indications that the matter was receiving attention far beyond the academic level.

In March 1990, we were pleased to learn that Vladimir Azhazha had been appointed as the head of the new All-Union Inter-Industrial Ufological Scientific Research Coordination Center affiliated with the Academy of Sciences.

In recent months the British journal *Flying Saucer Review* has begun to publish excellent translations of current Soviet reports from the Yaroslav region and other areas. UFO sightings are increasingly reported from the Ukraine and Siberia. And several U.S. government organizations, notably the Air Force's Foreign Technology Division (where Project Blue Book was located until it was shut down in 1969) and the Foreign Broadcast Information Service, have started issuing accurate and timely translations of Soviet UFO reports in their "Daily SNAP" and in *Foreign Press Note*.

These developments give us hope that a fruitful, long-term dialogue might be opening at last between researchers in the Soviet Union and their Western counterparts. For it is only through such dialogue that the UFO mystery will eventually be solved.

APPENDIX 1

A PRELIMINARY CATALOG OF SOVIET UFO SIGHTINGS

In the body of this book I have highlighted some forty cases that were specifically discussed during my stay in the Soviet Union in 1990. However, many other Soviet UFO incidents—such as the following events extracted from Professor Felix Zigel's works—have found their way into the literature and deserve to be mentioned, if only in summary form. Those researchers with an interest in digging further will also find good translations of Russian reports in the pages of the *Flying Saucer Review*,[41] whose editors are in regular contact with various Soviet investigative groups. The selection given below emphasizes the early years of the phenomenon, notably the 1967 wave, with a sample of reports prior to 1947.

July 1923. Dawn. Sosnovka
M. Volosnikov, who was on a steamship sailing along the Vyatka river in the vicinity of this village, saw an object resembling a flying moon. He followed its course for two or three minutes. The object turned to the right and disappeared. The witnesses compared notes and concluded it must be an "evil spirit."

Summer 1927. Early afternoon. Solovyevka
In this town which is located about thirteen miles south of Lipetsk, I.V. Surkov, an engineer, saw a white, milky disk in the northern sky. It was twice as large as the moon, flying slowly to the east. The weather was hot, with many cumulus clouds. *When the disk approached a cloud, the latter gradually disappeared, returning after it had passed.* This happened with every cloud along the disk's trajectory. The observation lasted for at least half an hour.

August 1933 or 1934. Kranye Chetay
V.N. Bronyukov and other children were playing in the street when they saw a "star" moving in the sky to the south, on an east-west trajectory, with the approximate speed of one of today's satellites. It changed course and flew to the northwest. It was observed for a total of ten minutes.

September 1935. Evening. Moscow
A. Ignatveya twice saw a strange phenomenon near the Petroskiy Gate. It was an illuminated sphere which flew low from north to south, fast and silently, on a horizontal trajectory.

Summer 1938. Early morning. Malakhovka oil station
N.A. Gosteva saw an object rushing close to him as he felt a light breeze. The phenomenon was a grayish white cloud, dense with diffuse outlines, oval in shape, larger than a zeppelin. The object emitted a distinct whistling sound.

September 1949. At night. Suzdal
A man who lived in a village about fifteen miles north of Suzdal, and many members of the collective farm where he worked, saw an object resembling an automobile headlight hovering above the village. *On one occasion it came close to the ground.* Three people, including G.A. Podoshivin, saw this phenomenon independently on the road between Suzdal and Gavrilovo-Posadskiy. It was yellowish green,

about half the lunar disk in apparent size, and it was spinning. It seemed to be located about one mile away. It vanished and reappeared several times, at ten-minute intervals.

November 1958. Sunset. Otyasskiy forest, Sosnovskiy rayon
Boris S. Khmyrov saw an object flying at high altitude from west to east. As it approached the zenith a disk suddenly appeared near it and it began to move fast in the opposite direction. Khmyrov saw the same disk again over the next several days.

January 1959. 07:00 Tobilsk
V.A. Golenkov saw *a brightly twinkling greenish star with sharp beams* or "rays" radiating from it. It became surrounded with bright fog, forming a spherical cloud, no larger than the full moon. It moved with constant speed and direction and it emitted a small star that went through a similar maneuver. The phenomenon lasted twenty minutes.

April 25, 1959. 06:00 Salizharovo Station near Kalinin
Aviation engineer Alexander B. Kadachev and his father were hunting at dawn when they saw an elliptical object with an aspect ratio of one third between its vertical and horizontal axes. It was dark, opaque but not completely black. Its lower edge was purple, perhaps because of its illumination by the rising sun. Its apparent diameter was approximately that of the moon. It was observed for several minutes. The witnesses lost sight of it as they walked through the forest but saw it again later, hovering higher in the sky.

July 6, 1960. 90 minutes after sunset. Teli (Tuvinskaya oblast)
A bright disk similar to the moon was observed in the west. It moved up and to the north with a speed of ten degrees in fifteen minutes, at an angle of forty-five degrees to the

horizon. Its diameter increased and its surface brightness decreased as it did so. The observation lasted thirty minutes. A group of eight people, including A.D. Danilov, senior scientist of the institute of applied geophysics in Moscow, saw the phenomenon.

July 8, 1960. Kamchuk River, 27 miles west of Teli
The same group of people involved in the July 6 observation saw a luminous disk again. It appeared from behind some mountains in the west. The weather was clear and cloudless. The region is unpopulated taiga.

Summer 1960. 17:00 Moscow
Many people, including a scientist named Golubov, saw *a rectangular yellow object* hovering above the city in the clear, windless, dark blue sky. It seemed to be at an altitude of several miles and "what held it there was completely incomprehensible." It was observed for over fifteen minutes.

Mid-August 1960. 22:00 Kuybyshev
V.N. Govorona was in a park when she saw a disk moving slowly across the sky. Its apparent size was smaller than that of the moon.

August 16, 1960. 23:00 Barakhudzir River
At a field camp situated eleven miles north of Koktal a party of geologists (including Nikolai A. Voroshilov, geochemist, Yevgeniy A. Sizov, geophysicist, Nikolai N. Sochevanov, geophysicist and Viktor N. Tulin, geologist) saw a luminous body moving from north to south above the mountains of the eastern slope. Its diameter was 1.2 times to 1.5 times the apparent diameter of the moon. It disappeared behind one of the peaks and reappeared on the other side before it was hidden from view again. It was white in color and very bright, round with some vertical elongation. There was no trail or afterglow. The sky was clear with only a few clouds.

October 1960. 23:00 Berk-Bisk, Biyal River
Engineer Y.M. Novikov was with a group of fifty people when they saw a lone dark cloud in a clear sky. The cloud was illuminated by a weak reddish light and *a beam of light slowly emerged from it.* It came from a solid body that separated from the cloud but continued to illuminate it with its beam. The phenomenon was observed for five minutes.

October 26, 1962. 23:40 Tula
Artist Y. Krivtsov and his companions were returning from a concert in Laptevo when they suddenly saw "eight or ten" objects flying north at an altitude of about 3,000 feet. They were of large size, hiding portions of the night sky. They flew horizontally in silence.

March 1964. 23:00 Petropavlovsk
Air Force reserve officer S.N. Popov was with three other men when he saw two strange disks moving one behind the other, then re-forming and moving as a pair. Passing almost over the witnesses, the disks emitted an intense bluish violet light. *When they were caught in the illumination from the disks, Popov and his companions felt oppressed, "as if some natural calamity had occurred, a very unpleasant feeling . . ."*

July 27, 1964. 22:00 Ulan Bator
Bold Khaserdzne, a worker with the Mongolian Chamber of Commerce, accompanied by a group of students, was travelling in a truck when they saw a moon-shaped object rising in the northwest. It climbed very rapidly for several minutes, getting larger in the process. It made a ninety-degree turn and flew north along the horizon for ten to fifteen minutes. After that it went down and disappeared.

November 30, 1964. 15:00 U.T. Shamakhinskiy Observatory, Azerbaijan
Astronomers M. Gadshiyev and K. Gusev saw an object moving from west to north at about one degree per minute.

The head of this object was about twice the diameter of the moon. It looked like a ring with a sharp internal edge and a diffuse outer edge. In the center was a star like object which was a point even when seen through a telescope. It left a tail that was visible for over fifteen minutes. No sound was heard.

August 12, 1965. 14:00 Liepaya, Latvia
V. Y. Leya, a glider pilot (later chief engineer on an aviation project) and several other pilots saw an oblate sphere, brilliant white, about half the size of the moon. It went through an arc of one hundred degrees.

February or March 1966. 08:00 Saranpul
At a place located some twelve miles northeast of Saranpul, at about 4,200 feet altitude, geologist I.N. Almazov and his coworkers observed two luminous objects practically overhead against the background of a cloudless sky. The first object was round, bright, yellow-white in color. The second object resembled the moon but was half the moon's apparent size. It became cloudy and smokelike, then changed to a bright illuminated disk. *On two occasions this second object emitted divergent beams like those of a car, for about half a minute each time.* Both objects moved to the northeast and disappeared behind a mountain.

April 4, 1966. Night. Region of Odessa
During night flights a radar operator checking his equipment discovered blips moving at approximately 500 miles per hour at 150,000 feet, dropping to 90,000 feet in fifteen minutes, then to 75,000 feet in thirty minutes, then to 54,000 feet in forty minutes, after which the phenomenon dropped to ground level. The data was confirmed by a ground radar station in Tiraspol, according to N.A. Baydukov.

June 16, 1966. 21:45 Elista
A detachment of scientists from the Volgograd oil and gas

research institute saw an object somewhat larger than a satellite, reddish in color, moving from the northeast to the southwest. Suddenly it dropped along a helical trajectory, taking a bright blue color. Something like an explosion occurred and a bright blue round cloud formed in its place. There was no sound, no other clouds and the stars were visible through the object.

Late July 1966. Midnight. Near Voronezh
Mr. and Mrs. Nikiforov saw a pulsating red disk moving at low altitude and at relatively low speed for five minutes.

Summer 1966. 09:00 Yuchka
A witness named N.Y. Marsov was bathing in the Kubek River when people called his attention to a shining ball in the sky. *Clouds dissipated when they came in the vicinity of the sphere.* It remained fixed in the sky for three hours.

July 18, 1966. 03:00 Rechport
Lidia Pavlovna Iliana, a senior spectroscopist of the central laboratory of the Berezovskaya expedition, and a bulldozer operator named F.A. Chesnokov, saw an orange disk in the sky. It was less bright than the moon but comparable to it in size. It was accompanied by several strange clouds. The phenomenon was observed for thirty minutes.

October 20, 1966. 15:00 Kherson
Walking back from the stadium to the bus station after a volleyball game, V.I. Duginov noticed that all the people in line were watching something in the sky. It was a round disk directly overhead, about one third the diameter of the moon. It had a soft silvery color and looked like a pearl or a bead but did not resemble a radiosonde or a balloon. It moved steadily to the east.

May 11, 1967. 21:10 Near Sheremetyevo airport
M.A. Selavnya and his father were walking the dogs on a sunny, warm evening with excellent visibility when they

heard a sound like a rustling that turned to a whistle and a rumble that passed over *as if coming from an invisible flying object.*

May 17, 1967. 02:30 Chapayevka
I.S. Rybak saw a round spot, about four times larger than the moon, with a faint luminous appearance like the Milky Way. It moved from west to east and was observed for thirty minutes.

May 17, 1967. 03:55 Ust'kamenogorsk
An engineer named T.N. Kanshov saw a bright body twice as large as the moon moving across the sky from south to north for over two minutes. It first appeared as a flame so bright he could read the time on his watch by its light. The night was quiet, cloudless, moonless. The object had "fiery arrows" extending parallel to its sides. It expanded to three times its original size before disappearing.

May 17, 1967. 22:00 Kamyshin
Major Y.B. Popov, of Novosibirsk, together with Junior Lieutenant A.S. Nikitenko and several local residents saw a cascade of lights rushing across the night sky from the northeast in even rows. The lights were located on the surface of a very large cigar-shaped object: *the impression was that an ocean-going vessel was flying across the sky with absolute silence* at an altitude of about 0.6 mile. It was observed for two or three minutes. It passed almost overhead and took off into space.

May 17, 1967. 22:05 Bakhrushev
By a warm, quiet evening several witnesses including S.V. Ostrovskiy saw a bright point descending in the western sky. It flew down to an altitude estimated as about one mile, when it changed to a horizontal course. At that point it appeared as a dark body of impressive proportions, with a compact, well-defined light at the rear. It flew off silently at less than 200 mph, with a dark orange tail behind it.

Early June 1967. 23:00 Khoper River
While walking along the banks of the river M. Gavrilyuk and his wife saw a luminous object shaped like a half moon. The weather was clear and the real moon was shining in the sky. The object moved from the west to the south, passing above the moon and accelerating until it disappeared, leaving a faint trace.

July 4, 1967. 21:15 Shakhty
Docent Y. Krasuntsev and his son were resting near the Don River when they saw a half moon shaped object. They first noticed two luminous points that looked like artificial satellites. They moved to the southeast, making no sound. A shower of orange sparks flew out of one object and turned into a moon shape that went on flying.

July 8, 1967. 23:00 Volgograd
Dr. Boris Dikhedeyev and a companion were talking outside when they saw an orange object in the form of a half moon. It moved from west to east, leaving a trail that disappeared in the rear and appeared in front of the object as it flew toward the forest. The moon was shining and the sky was clear.

July 8, 1967. 21:30 Romny
By a quiet evening S.V. Zazulya and his wife saw an object flying from north to south. It looked like an ordinary cloud but flew very fast and above the few high fleecy clouds that were in the sky.

July 10, 1967. 23:00 Krugloye, Shakhterskiy
A.A. Podgorny was coming back from the movies when he saw an object shaped like a half moon flying from south to north. Three days later he saw the same phenomenon again.

July 16, 1967. 21:00 Kudepst
V.N. Chernyavski and his wife, with N. Ognevoy and S. Voronov, were close to the shore when they saw a yellow-

rose disk-shaped object moving from west to east in the sky from the direction of the sea. It passed behind some clouds. The witness had the time to take a two-kopek coin from his pocket and he observed that the coin covered the object exactly when held at arm's length.

July 17, 1967. 23:00 Sukhumi (Agudzeri)
L.V. Antonova, an editor with the publishing house *Thought*, and T.I. Dantseva, fellow of the Kurchatov scientific institute, observed a strange object along with four other people. The weather was clear at the time. The object looked like a flat disk with shining edge, flying at an altitude of some 350 feet at the speed of a propeller aircraft.

July 18, 1967. 14:47 Amvrosiyevka
Student Y. Divak and a friend were fishing when they saw the reflection of a strange flying object in the water. Looking up, they saw a lusterless craft in the sky. It seemed to affect the sounds from the trains and from the nearby town.

July 31, 1967. 21:15 Privilny farm, Kavkazkiy
I. Kosov, his wife and farmer P.I. Marchenko saw a dark red disk flying from the southwest to the northeast. The witness had time to count to forty-two before the object disappeared.

August 2, 1967. 23:30 Norwegian Sea
A Soviet vessel, the *Izhevsk*, was sailing west with Captain Markov, senior engineer Ivanov and first assistant captain Bazhanin in the cabin when the navigator, Sysoyev, reported a strange phenomenon in the sky. Going to the bridge, they all saw a white sphere moving south. Several minutes later another bright spot was seen high in the sky, increasing in size and emitting bright colors in which yellow was dominant. This phenomenon was repeated several times.

August 5, 1967. 20:50 Perm
Y.G. Solovyev, his wife and his son observed a ring-shaped

object flying across the sky. An airliner flying at an altitude of 1,200 feet would have fit inside this ring. It was observed for over ten minutes in the western part of the sky.

August 8, 1967. 20:40 Kislovodsk
An object shaped like a sharply outlined asymmetrical crescent flew over the mountain astronomical station of the Academy of Sciences. The object was slightly smaller than the moon, about twenty minutes of arc, with a color described as reddish by some observers, yellow for others. It flew from west to east about twenty degrees above the horizon, moving from the Big Dipper to Cassiopeia in about thirty seconds, at a uniform speed. *The witnesses were A.A. Sazonov, a specialist in the ionosphere; V.A. Tsion of the Leningrad Polytechnical Institute, and seven members of a biological expedition.*

About August 9, 1967. 15:00 Belye Krinitsy
Mr. Lytkiny and his wife were on vacation, resting by the shore of a lake, when they saw a fast-moving oval object. It was milky white, with some small black rods arranged randomly on its surface. It suddenly moved sharply to the right and up, then to the left and downward. It then resumed its continuous path toward the Carpathians. A few minutes later a second object appeared and went through similar evolutions.

August 30, 1967. 20:50 Dneprodzerzhinsk
A round, bright, uniformly illuminated light yellow disk was seen describing a wide arc in the sky. It disappeared to the north-northeast. Mr. V.M. Chernov saw it through binoculars for a while as it went behind some clouds and reappeared, fainter and looking like a greenish star. There was no sound.

September 2, 1967. 23:35 Pechora
Four people, including physicist Mikhail F. Zherebin, saw a “mistiness” in the north-northwestern part of the sky.

Suddenly it changed into a clear yellow disk comparable in size to the full moon (which was also in the sky). A yellow flash occurred and the disk turned orange. The phenomenon was observed for twelve minutes.

September 4, 1967. 21:17 Yevpatoriya
N.N. Pronin, senior editor with the *Mysl* publishing house in Moscow, accompanied by his wife, saw a white, crescent-shaped object fly over from the northeast to the southwest along a straight line at an altitude of about 2,500 feet. The object moved with the convex part facing forward. The weather was clear.

September 9, 1967. 20:20 Donetsk
A witness reported a concave flying object, the color of molten metal, accompanied by a bright "star." The phenomenon moved from south to east.

September 19, 1967. 19:40 Belgogradskaya
A witness named A. Serdyukov, who was travelling with a group of communications technicians, observed a luminous half-moon rising high in the sky directly in front of them. It descended rapidly, leaving a cone-shaped tail. The men stopped their vehicles to watch it. *After about forty seconds the half-moon appeared to swing in the sky, becoming smaller in size, as its color turned to red.* It assumed a drop-like shape and stopped, hanging in the sky for a minute, after which it seemed to dissolve.

Early October 1967. Noon. Sukhumi
Engineer V.N. Chechyanov and his coworkers saw a strange object in the clear blue sky for half an hour. It hovered for a while, then moved along the shore, rose and disappeared. *A man who watched it through binoculars reported that the object was shaped like a triangle,* with no fuselage and no tail, and was the color of aluminum.

October 18, 1967. 21:00 Dzhubga
A Moscow physician who was visiting this town saw a

bright object with the shape of a sphere moving evenly from the sea toward the east. The crowd attending an open-air movie projection witnessed the occurrence as well.

October 18, 1967. 18:00 Pyatigorsk
Astronomer Z. Kadikov, from Kazan Engelgardt observatory, saw a bright object in the northwest. It was a crescent with sharp edges and pointed horns, yellow in color with a pale bluish tail, moving at about 1.5 degrees per second. It became smaller as it flew and was eventually reduced to a point. *Finding other witnesses, Kadikov was able to triangulate the phenomenon.* He estimated it may have been about fifty miles above the earth and some 1,800 feet between the "horns," flying at about three miles per second.

October 25, 1967. 16:05 Otradnoy Stanista
Witness N. Savrasov, an advanced geography student, and his mother-in-law were able to observe two spherical objects flying from the northwest to the southeast. The largest object was yellowish, cloudy. The smaller one, which seemed to be pulling it, appeared metallic.

November 6, 1967. Night. Kazan
Mr. and Mrs. Masgutov saw an object shaped like the planet Saturn, a luminous reddish sphere with a flat ring of the same color, which hovered for some seven to ten minutes, spinning on its axis. It gradually increased its speed and disappeared.

November 9, 1967. Miass, near Chelyabin
A white cigar-shaped object with some black dashes at one end was seen moving through the sky by I.S. Lunyanov. It was flying toward Zlatoust.

November 14, 1967. Liepaya
A large, luminous object shaped like a hemisphere hovered low over the ground. It moved away quickly with a fiery light that was painful to the eye. There were several witnesses.

November 15, 1967. 04:30 Sasnava
V. Treychis observed a round object in the sky for thirty-five minutes, twenty degrees above the northeast horizon. It seemed to measure 300 feet in diameter. It was very bright and tongues of flame were visible.

November 25, 1967. Midnight. Mikhaylovka
V. Rogov was listening to the radio inside his home when a bright green light called his attention outside. He saw an object flying at great speed across the sky. It disappeared like a meteor but it then reappeared on the same trajectory. *It was round and flat, with bright edges.* The phenomenon lasted ten minutes.

APPENDIX 2

CASE INDEX

Good science is a science of measurement. The UFO phenomenon cannot be studied without the application of a systematic classification system, together with a measure of each case's reliability. Just as stellar astronomy stagnated until Hertzprung and Russell produced their classic diagram based on the color-luminosity classification, UFO research cannot get anywhere until its practitioners recognize the need for a solid taxonomy that can be reliably applied.

The following index to Soviet UFO cases uses a complete classification system I have proposed in my earlier book *Confrontations*. For clarity the major concepts of the system will be reviewed here.

ANOMALIES AND CLOSE ENCOUNTERS

In order to encompass the full range of phenomena one finds in the modern literature, it is important to acknowledge that UFOs are related in significant ways to other events. It is the rule, rather than the exception, to find significant UFO sightings preceded or followed by anomalies, notably of the poltergeist variety.

For that reason, I have found it useful to begin with a classification of anomalies into four groups that parallel Dr. J. Allen Hynek's close encounter categories:

AN1 are anomalies that do not have lasting physical effects, such as amorphous lights or unexplained explosions.

AN2 are anomalies with lasting physical effects, such as some poltergeist phenomena, apports (objects reportedly materializing out of thin air), and areas of flattened grass.

AN3 are anomalies with associated entities. This class could include reports of ghosts, yetis, and other instances of crypto-zoology, as well as elves and spirits.

AN4 are those anomalous reports in which witnesses experienced personal interaction with entities in the reality of the entities themselves. They include near-death experiences, religious miracles and visions, and many cases of out-of-body experiences.

Finally, I place under the AN5 category the cases of anomalous injuries or deaths, such as spontaneous combustion or unexplained wounds. I also place here the cases of permanent healing often described in the literature of the paranormal.

We now come to the UFO reports themselves, which I will divide, following Hynek, into close encounters and distant sightings.

I see no reason to change anything to the classification of close encounters that is in current use, from CE1 to CE4, although Hynek himself was not responsible for creating the CE4 category and was not especially happy with it. In recent years the need has become acute for a new category, CE5, that will encompass cases of close encounters in which the witnesses have suffered permanent injuries or other physiological effects.

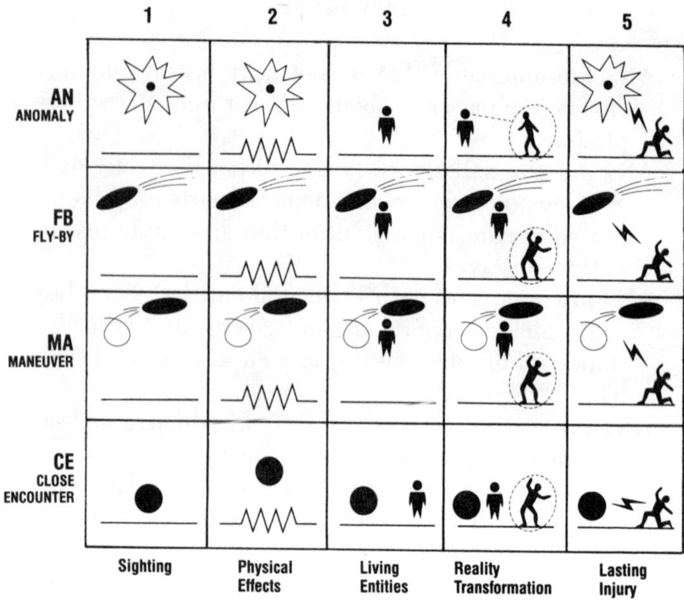

Fig. 10. Classification of anomalies related to UFOs.

MANEUVERS AND FLYBYS

The distant sightings, in my view, are best classified according to the apparent behavior of the object rather than circumstances independent of it, such as daylight or night, or radar rather than visual observation. Accordingly, I have found it useful to introduce two general categories: MA (Maneuvers) and FB (Flyby). Within these categories I have tried to give definitions that were parallel to those of close encounters:

MA1 gathers those UFO observations that involve an object with a discontinuous trajectory (such as a drop, a maneuver, or a loop).

MA2 includes those cases that give rise to physical effects in addition to a discontinuous trajectory.
MA3 contains the cases of objects with discontinuous trajectories when beings are observed on board.
MA4 covers instances of maneuvers accompanied by a sense of transformation of reality for the percipient.
MA5 is a maneuver as a result of which the witnesses suffer significant injury or death.

Similarly, the flyby events are classified into five categories:

FB1 is a simple sighting of a UFO flying by in the sky, the category most frequently reported.
FB2 is a flyby accompanied by physical evidence.
FB3 is a flyby of an object accompanied by the observation of beings on board.
FB4 is a flyby in which the witness experienced a transformation of his or her reality into the reality of the object or its occupants.
FB5 is a flyby as a result of which the witnesses would suffer significant injuries.

THE SVP CREDIBILITY RATING

No classification system is complete without a method of assigning credibility or weight to an observation. While such a procedure is an integral part of any intelligence evaluation task, UFO researchers have rarely bothered to apply it in support of their own work. It is important to implement a system that is simple enough to be applied quickly and easy enough to be remembered so that it does not require constant reference to a manual or set of tables.

In my own work I now use a three-digit code to indicate

the weight of a UFO case. Each of the three digits has a value from 0 to 4, as follows:

FIRST DIGIT: SOURCE RELIABILITY (S)

0 Unknown source or unreliable source
1 Report attributed to a known source of uncalibrated reliability
2 Reliable source, secondhand
3 Reliable source, firsthand
4 Firsthand personal interview with the witness by a source of proven reliability

SECOND DIGIT: SITE VISIT (V)

0 No site visit, or answer unknown
1 Site visit by a casual person not familiar with such phenomena
2 Site visit by persons familiar with such phenomena
3 Site visit by a reliable investigator with some experience
4 Site visit by a skilled analyst

THIRD DIGIT: POSSIBLE EXPLANATIONS (P)

0 Data consistent with one or more natural causes
1 Natural explanation requires only slight modification of the data
2 Natural explanation requires gross alteration of one parameter
3 Natural explanation requires gross alteration of several parameters
4 No natural explanation possible, given the evidence

INDEX OF CASES CITED

LOCATION	TYPE	SVP	DATE	TIME	REGION	WITNESSES
Baskushak	MA5	444	16-06-1948		Caspian	Apraksin
Cabanas	CE5	444	14-06-1968	00:05	Cuba	Puentes
Cabardino	MA1	334	13-02-1989	21:00	Caucasus	Thousands
Cape Kamenny	FB1	444	03-12-1967		Arctic	Airliner
Chekhov	CE2	444	07-1977	day	Serpukhov	Three men
Cherepovets	MA1	113	24-04-1989	22:55	Vologda	Veselova
Dalnegorsk	AN2	441	29-01-1986		Siberia	Multiple
Erenin	FB1	444	13-02-1989			Pilots
Gagra	MA1	443	19-09-1968	20:00	Black Sea	Unknown
Kalinin	AN3	443	1933		Russia	Zolotov
Kiev	CE3	444	04-07-1989	18:00	Ukraine	Women
Konantsevo	CE3	113	06-06-1989		Vologda	Children
Lake Onega	CE2	444	27-04-1961	morng	Leningrad	Multiple
Minsk	MA5	444	07-09-1984	04:10	Bielorussia	Pilots
Moscow	FB1	332	31-07-1982		Russia	Multiple
Moscow	MA2	333	08-1974		Russia	Multiple
Nalchik	CE4	333	11-10-1989	18:00	Caucasus	Woman
Nicolayev	CE4	334	16-09-1989	24:00	Ukraine	Woman
Octobriski	CE2	444	04-1967		Bakhiri	
Perm	AN3	113	Summer 89	04:30	Urals	Medvedev
Perm	CE4	443	06-02-1989	night	Urals	Woman
Perm	AN3	443	04-1986		Urals	Bachurin
Perm	AN3	442	06-1987		Urals	One man
Perslavl	MA1	443	21-03-1990	22:05	Moscow	Semenchen
Roboziero	MA5	444	15-08-1663	12:00	Bieloziero	Fiedorov

LOCATION	TYPE	SVP	DATE	TIME	REGION	WITNESSES
Rostov/Don	FB1	333	18-10-1967	17:00	S.Russia	Alferov
Saratov	MA2	444	06-05-1949		Volga	Apraksin
Shamakinsky	FB1	444	30-11-1964	18:00	Azerbaijan	Gusev
Shevchenko	FB1	113	01-09-1989		Caspian Sea	Unknown
Solnechnogsk	CE4	444	21-07-1975	15:00	Russia	Malichev
Turgay	CE2	333	late 06-79		Kazakhstan	Multiple
Tunguska	AN2	442	30-06-1908	07:00	Siberia	Semenov
Ulyanovsk	AN3	443	1986	morng	Kazan	Mr. N.
Usovo	MA2	444	31-07-1969	20:00	Moscow	Tseknovch
Vologda	MA1	113	11-06-1989	21:20	Vologda	O.Lubnina
Voronezh	CE3	444	21-09-1989		Russia	Lukin
Voronezh	CE3	444	23-09-1989	21:00	Russia	Torshin
Voronezh	FB1	443	24-09-1989	22:30	Russia	Kugatov
Voronezh	CE3	444	27-09-1989	18:30	Russia	Surin
Voronezh	FB1	334	27-09-1989	19:00	Russia	Malveyev
Voronezh S.	CE2	444	late 09-89		Russia	Polyakov
Voronezh	FB1	444	29-09-1989	20:10	Russia	Yatsunov

NOTES

1. Associated Press dispatch, 8 October 1989.
2. *Waterbury Republican*, 10 October 1989.
3. *Hartford Courant*, 11 October 1989.
4. Howard Blum, *Out There* (New York: Simon & Schuster, 1990).
5. *Newsweek*, 23 October 1989, 42.
6. *San Francisco Chronicle*, 10 October 1989.
7. "Tass's Thrill—Joking Over U.F.O. Report," *New York Times*, 12 October 1989.
8. Martine Castello's article on the New Age in America appeared in *Figaro Madame*, 27 January 1990, 84.
9. See Jacques Vallee's previous books on the subject of UFO research, notably his recent trilogy on alien contact: *Dimensions* (Chicago: Contemporary Books, 1988), *Confrontations* (New York: Ballantine, 1990), and *Revelations* (New York: Ballantine, 1991).
10. Martine Castello and Isabelle Blanc have written a book about the UMMO question, *La Conspiration des Etoiles* (Paris: Laffont, 1991).
11. Professor Vladimir Azhazha is the author of *Hydronauts* (Moscow: Znanie, 1964) and of several articles about oceanography, notably "New Achievements in the Field of Deep Submarine Diving" (1965), "Problems in the Theory and Application of Hydroacoustical

Sciences" (1966), and "Use of Submarines for Scientific Purposes" (*Nauka i Zhizn*, 1969).

12. James Oberg, "The Russian Connection," *Omni*, July 1980.
13. Jacques Vallee, "Five Arguments Against the Extraterrestrial Origin of Unidentified Flying Objects," *Journal of Scientific Exploration* 4, no. 1 (1990): 105–117.
14. "A Football Game with Aliens," *Voronezh Kommuna*, 3 October 1989.
15. "What Was It?" *Voronezh Kommuna*, 7 October 1989.
16. *Izvestia*, 12 October 1989.
17. *Selskaya Zhizn*, 11 October 1989.
18. "They Fly . . . ," *Molodoy Kommunar*, 12 October 1989.
19. *Meditsinskaya Gazeta*, 5 October 1989.
20. A. V. Zolotov, *Problema Tunguskoi Katastrophi 1908* (Minsk: Science and Technique, 1969).
21. Among the numerous publications in English about the Tunguska explosion, see Jack Stovely, *Cauldron of Hell* (London: W. H. Allen/Starbook, 1977); John Baxter and Thomas Atkins, *The Fire Came By* (New York: Warner Books, 1976); and Rupert Furneaux, *The Tungus Event* (St. Albans: Panther/Granada, 1977).
22. Alexander Kazantsev, *A Visitor From Outer Space* (Moscow: Foreign Languages Publishing House, n.d.).
23. Felix Zigel was the author of numerous scientific articles, notably "Radio Waves From Outer Space" (*Detgiz*, 1963), "Inhabitable Worlds" (*Znanie*, 1962), "Nuclear Explosion Over the Taiga" (*Ananlye-Sila*, 1961), and "Unusual Galaxies" (*Iun. Tekh.*, 1960), as well as several publications for science and astronomy teachers.
24. Henry Gris and William Dick, *Les Nouveaux Sorciers du Kremlin* (Paris: Tchou, 1979).
25. Ion Hobana and Julien Weverbergh, *Les OVNI en URSS* (Paris: Robert Laffont, 1976).

26. Henry Kamm, "A Soviet Astronomer Suggests World Study of Flying Saucers," *New York Times*, 10 December 1967.
27. Based on an interview of Vladimir Krat by Ilya Fonyakov, *Literaturnaya Gazeta*, 26 July 1978, 13.
28. From an article in *Nedelya* no. 3 (January 15–21, 1979): 8–9.
29. Alexander Kazantsev and Jacques Vallee, "What Is Flying in Our Skies?" *Young Technology Magazine*, no. 8 (1965) and *Trud*, 24 August 1967.
30. Jacques Vallee, *The Invisible College* (New York: E. P. Dutton, 1975).
31. Jacques Vallee, *Messengers of Deception* (Berkeley, Calif.: And/Or Press, 1979) and (New York: Bantam, 1980).
32. Historical archives collected and published by the archaeological commission, part IV, St. Petersburg, 1842.
33. Felix Zigel, *Unidentified Flying Objects in the USSR*, privately printed (February 1968).
34. *Rabochaya Tribuna*, 19 April 1990.
35. Emil Bachurin, *Commentaries on "Passport to Magonia,"* privately printed (1988).
36. A typical photograph of the northern lights (aurora borealis) can be found in *Sky and Telescope* (July 1990): 105. Taken by Pekka Parviainen of Finland, it is practically identical to the *Novosti* photograph of alleged "energy fields in the Perm region."
37. See John Derr and Michael Persinger, "Luminous Energy and Seismic Energy in the Central United States," *Journal of Scientific Exploration* 4, no. 1 (1990): 55; and Paul Devereux, *Earthlights* (Wellingborough: Turnstone Press, 1982).
38. L. M. Gindilis, D. A. Menkov, and I. G. Petrovskaya, "Observations of Anomalous Atmospheric Phenomena in the USSR: Statistical Analysis," USSR Academy of Sciences, Institute of Space Research Report PR 473

(1979): 1–74. Translated by NASA as Technical Memorandum no. 75665 (February 1980).

39. Claude Poher and Jacques Vallee, "Basic Patterns in UFO Observations," AIAA no. 75-42 (Paper delivered at the Thirteenth AIAA Aerospace Science Meeting, Pasadena, Calif., 20 January 1975).
40. The Law of the Times was first described in detail in *Challenge to Science* by Jacques and Janine Vallee (Chicago: Regnery, 1966).
41. The *Flying Saucer Review* can be obtained from: P.O. Box 162, High Wycombe, Bucks, HP13 50Z, England.

INDEX